ALIEN COMMANDERS RELUCTANT BRIDE

DRACONIAN WARRIORS BOOK 3

JUNO WELLS

CONTENTS

PROLOGUE

*M*any thousands of years ago, deep in the Exion star system the first Draconian female entered the Cave of Ascension. She passed through the softly glowing waters, noticing tiny luminous blobs moving about in the water. Whether they were finless fish or worms was difficult to tell, for they had the characteristics of both, as well as thin filaments growing out of their frail bodies.

Knowing the cave must be her divine destiny, the first queen forced herself to submit to the will of the gods. She walked slowly through the glowing waters, emerging a queen on the other side. Her people were equal parts awed and terrified when she disappeared beneath the eerie luminescent liquid, for none had dared to pass through the glowing waters before.

When she took her rightful place as leader of her people, all was well for a brief time. Soon her sleep became restless. A suspicion crept forward from the back of her mind as she felt something strange growing in her body. It moved around and playfully tickled her insides. Since she had no fever, nor evidence of disease upon her skin, horns or wings, the healers assured her that all was well. Then the nightmares started, and she never knew a moment's peace thereafter. Every day was a struggle to shut out the dark voice growing ever stronger in her mind. Once the symbiont took full control of her faculties, the young woman was forced to stand idly by while the creature wreaked havoc on her people.

From that day to this, every Draconian female had been forced to walk through the Waters of Ascension, thus becoming a queen in her own right. The evil of the cave was disguised as a coming of age ceremony for young females and the Draconian were taught to love this sacred rite, thus perpetuating the age of the symbiont. The first symbiont was long-lived, and few knew it still wandered the verse looking for plunder and warriors. Most warriors prayed to never meet the elder queens, for they were much more vicious than younger queens. Their dedication to terrifying and torturing males was legendary.

As the decades flew by, the queens grew discontented, fought amongst themselves and battled with each other over warriors. They seemed to grow stronger, crave chaos and feed off the misery of others. Little did the Draconians know, but the creatures were not a strange anomaly, born of their planet, but rather the spawn of a soul sucker that had been driven from a nearby world.

Meanwhile on Earth, the environment was deteriorating, turning the oceans into putrid acidic cesspools, devoid of all life forms. The lives of many males were lost in an effort to clean up the contamination, and then the worst-case scenario came to pass. A new pathogen emerged and locked onto the male genome. It took time to develop an antigen, costing more lives still. By the time it was all said and done, the ratio of males to females was seriously unbalanced, there being four females to every male.

Just when humans were losing hope, aliens made contact with the peoples of Earth. They kindly offered to help with the environmental disaster and provided much-needed medical supplies and foodstuffs. In return, the aliens requested the one thing Earth had a surplus of. Voluntary human brides were offered in exchange for the supplies. Many women were all too happy to relocate to a pristine new planet with an accommodating alien husband.

During transport to one of these alien worlds, women encountered the Draconian. The ever-curious humans discovered the truth about the symbionts, leaving the Draconian warriors grief-stricken. The dragon warriors had suffered long under the rule of symbionts and jumped at the chance to have human brides. Some even escaped the Exion star system using wormhole technology.

Only, the original ancient queen haunted their every step. Finding a new galaxy, she was intent upon exploiting it just as she had the last. Unfortunately for the ancient queen, she met her match in an equally brutal race of aliens called the Moltan. They promptly stripped her from her humanoid form and imprisoned her in a bubble of life-sustaining liquid. Without her humanoid shell, she was vulnerable enough to kill. Unfortunately, one can never be quite sure some of her genetic matter didn't survive to infect others.

Her once-captive Draconian males bump into remnants of their prehistoric queen when they least expect it. These are the stories of their struggle to survive and keep the symbionts from entering the new quadrant of space. Naxis was the name of their new quadrant and it offered a completely new way of life for the battle-hardened warriors.

Feeling of Impending Doom

~ Tabor ~

The youngster I'm accustomed to seeing joking around and asking a million questions has somehow been transformed into a warrior worthy of being taken seriously. Among the Dracon, older brothers take younger ones under their wings as they come of age. It is my honor to usher Phan into adulthood, for we are the only two brothers to survive the rule of Draconian queens.

Seeing him standing in a full warrior's uniform with his wings folded neatly behind him and his horns perked up makes me remember how much he coveted the dress of a warrior when he wore a junior warrior's uniform. The black uniform with the green piping of a healer looks good on him with his green skin.

We both look much like our sire, especially with our clade symbols inked down our right cheek, onto our shoulder, and right down to our finger tips. The clade of Salon is gifted with green scales, a huge wingspan, and the ability to sense our opponent's next move in combat. Every Draconian line has a gift, and ours lends itself to making fine security officers.

Standing at Phan's side is his best friend, Timric. The youth's long golden hair marks him out as a true breeder. It is fitting that they have chosen to become a fighting unit. It was the same with Timric's father and me in our youth. We were inseparable until Meric was chosen by his queen. Now his son, my brother and I will enjoy action and adventure while he nests with his queen. If being left behind on our new home world bothers him, Meric does not show it. Though I will miss him, my time has come to lead, and I am intent on enjoying the privilege.

We will leave for Denar Five shortly. This will be my first command mission and my brother's first mission as a sanctioned warrior. We're both keen on ensuring a successful operation. I've planned out our mission to the smallest detail. Since the sister queens will be under our protection, I've left nothing to chance.

This is one of the last training sessions before we leave. I watch the two young warriors select their weapons from the walls of our spacious training room. They choose the traditional weapon of our forefathers and converge on the mat to face each other. Others crowd around, for there are few warriors in their age group or class on this world. At the sound of the first chime, they drop into a traditional fighting stance with their batlets held in the correct defensive pose.

Pride swells in my chest as the second chime sounds and they attack each other with a vengeance reserved for warriors who thirst for blood. Phan spreads his wings. It's a risky move. On the one hand it makes him light on his feet and agile, but it also opens his wings to abuse from his opponent's batlet.

Timric wastes no time swiping at the tips of my brother's wings. My own best friend has taught his son well, as I have Phan. They are equally matched and it's truly fascinating to watch their strategy play out.

I notice something right away. While Timric's form is pure,

my brother has integrated human fighting techniques into his tactics. He's more aggressive than I remember him being as well. Though his fighting partner does not seem to notice, Phan has quantum leaped forward in fighting ability. My brother is clever, resourceful, and does not stand on ceremony. Excitement ripples around the room, as the other warriors press closer to get a better look.

When Timric is on his back with my brother's batlet at his throat, the room erupts in the thumping of warriors pounding on their chest plates in admiration. Phan steps back, and the warriors begin to speak. There is spirited conversation about integrating fighting moves from other species.

Timric scrambles to his feet with a huge smile on his face. Within moments, Phan is walking him though one of his new moves. Because I've known Timric all his life, I trust him to have my brother's back in battle.

A voice sounds off from nearby. "Your brother is wise in his own way, Tabor. You must be proud of him."

Sparing my fellow warrior a side glance, my wings tighten slightly. "I have always been proud of Phan. He is the only warrior among us fully trained in healing. However, I'm not sure about these new moves. Though effective, changing our fighting style feels like diluting our heritage."

The elder warrior is one I have known for many solars and his response gives me something to think about. "The 'verse is ever changing, commander. Those species unable to adapt get shoved to the dust bin of history. I have no wish to see that happen to our people. We have only very recently earned our freedom and the chance to have a mate of our own."

Turning to face Scarn, I respond respectfully. "Our lives are much different since entering the Naxis sector of space."

"Yet we have adapted to freedom and all that it entails. I feel for the first time that my life is truly worth living. We've gotten good at accepting change, and this sets us apart from many species.

Where they are reluctant to embrace new ideas, we are quick to explore and modify our approach to fighting, mating, and politics."

I smother back a smile. "I believe this is why the Intergalactic Council of Planets accepted us so easily. Our ability to cooperate and follow the law marked us out as honorable males and worthy allies."

The older man leans onto the thick railing of the catwalk and gazes at the warriors sparring below. They are all now practicing Phan's new moves. "We have found a paradise in this sector of space. There are no Draconian queens or symbionts to lord power over us, only sweet human queens who wear their emotions on their lovely faces for all to see."

"It is clear you have not met the sister queens. They are forever serious, and do not show their blunt little teeth to any warrior." Showing of teeth is a mating gesture, one that human females engage in often. The sister queens are the only ones who never show their teeth to males.

Scarn's head swivels around to look at me, his expression pensive for a brief moment. "I have thought this over many times. I believe there are many ways for a human queen to initiate mating rituals with a preferred warrior. The baring of teeth is our way, not their way."

"You sound like you have some experience luring a queen, my friend. If this is the case, you should share your newfound knowledge." The thought of this elder warrior with his own female gladdens my heart. He has suffered much at the hands of our former queens and deserves a tender touch in his old age. His quick response dashes any hope I had of him growing old with a mate of his own.

"Don't be ridiculous, Tabor. No human queen would choose a battle-scarred elder warrior for a mate." He goes back to watching the warriors spar. "Entares crafted their forms to be delicate and beautiful. By comparison I am monstrous. Therefore, I will leave the mating to younger males." His side glance in my direction reminds me that I am thought to be attractive.

"I am living proof that having a handsome face is no guarantee a queen will warm to a warrior. The goddess may have a crafted a pleasing exterior to house my soul, but that has earned me little notice by the human queens. It seems they require more than a pleasing countenance to look upon, Elder Scarn. They want males of worth. It makes me think you have as good a chance as any at luring a queen."

A grunt is all the response I get in return for what I intended to be positive encouragement. After a pause he murmurs, "Then look for signs of trust and admiration. Even the sister queens allow their emotions to show from time to time. Their expressions are simply less intense than other queens."

Deflated, I respond politely, "I will pay close attention to their responses. Thank you for your wise council this day, elder."

My compliment makes him smile slightly. The thin scars criss-crossing his face have been there for so long they seem to belong. I believe he would have been thought of as handsome in his day. His hand comes up to slap me jovially on the back. "Anytime you have need of my wisdom, you have only to call for me, commander." He swaggers off, apparently contented to pass on his wisdom.

Turning back to watch my warriors train, I look for weaknesses and areas for improvement. Elder Scarn is correct about adapting and integrating new ideas is one of our primary strengths in this new world.

I pull out my handheld and begin scrolling through the lists of supplies I have ordered for my upcoming mission to Denar Five. The sister queens have been working night and day in the gemstone mines. Uncertain why I've taken an interest in these particular queens, I've been adding to their stock when they are not present. However, there is only so much I can add without them noticing. They have made it clear they wish to earn independently so no one can lay claim to their venture. As if I would do such a thing. Their persistence and the frantic pace with which they work lead me to believe they have a greater need. I also went behind their back and made a deal with the tradesman who bought their gemstone to pay them far in excess of its value. I made up the excess in precious minerals culled from our home world, all to speed them on their way.

They care nothing about their own comfort. I see this clearly in their decision to wear plain uniforms and sleep under the stars. I hang around, stoke their fire, and add extra blankets over their small bodies to ward off the chill night air. When they began to gather crew, I was chosen to command their mission. I suspect it is because they have tolerated my hanging about, and in the process became comfortable with my presence. I in turn invited only the warriors I most trusted to speak to Queen Kearney about signing onto her crew. Most have been assisting me in digging for gemstone and minerals as well as gathering supplies. They are already vested in the success of the mission and wish for more action and adventure than our home world affords.

Something about the sister queens leaves worry squirming in my gut. It may be my family gift at work hinting at some danger we cannot yet see. Normally, my gift comes into play only during a battle, so I may be wrong on that accord. No matter how many times I tell myself the queens are safe and all is right, the feeling of impending doom only grows larger.

I click though our medical supplies, ensuring everything we could possibly need to treat a queen is stocked for this voyage. I have secured a sturdy tent to ensure their privacy and provide shelter from the elements. Stored away in my crates there is food, water, lighting, bedding, extra clothing, the aforementioned medical supplies and a wide assortment of tools to repair and maintain her ship. I have stocked my credit account with an astronomical sum. On the off chance that our mission goes terribly wrong, I can feed us and get everyone home with credits to spare.

I've covered all my bases, so why does the feeling of impending doom not ease? Movement across the catwalk catches my notice. When I glance up, my wings flutter in alarm. The two queens are standing on the other side of the room watching our warriors spar. Queen Kearney is wearing a flight suit covered in dust, alerting me that she has been in the gemstone mines again.

The younger queen is on her knees staring at Phan and Timric. Her eyes are moving around, tracking their every move, and her facial expression is thoroughly intrigued. The way she looks at my young brother sends a chill down my spine. Surely she is too young to select a mate. For certain, my brother is too young to be chosen. I sneak a peek down below, and realize she must have her eye on Timric. He is a true breeder and naturally his golden skin and hair would draw the notice of a queen over my brother's handsome face.

When I lift my eyes, Queen Kearney is staring at me. Her expression is totally blank, but she reaches out to put a hand on her sister's shoulder. Lowering my head, I take a step back. She doesn't want me seeing where her younger sister's eyes have strayed. It's not my concern if they wish to fold Timric into their family. He is young but a fine choice nonetheless.

esting Dolls

~ Kearney ~

Staring directly at the strange Draconian male who seems to have appointed himself our protector, I dare him to cast his eyes upon my sister that way again. Thankfully, he steps back. After darting a quick glance to the warriors down below, he melts back into the shadows. The last thing I see is the tattoo inked down the side of his face. It almost glows in the dark, giving off a sinister vibe.

Tabor's normally so matter-of-fact about taking care of us that I sometimes toy with the idea that he's just following someone else's orders to make sure we're fed and sheltered. He rarely looks us in the eye or spares us much face-to-face attention. He just goes about his day, and in the process, checks in on us regularly.

I'm guessing that in their world, Kendra and I are a bit of an anomaly. All the other women stay either at the luxurious apartment complex that's been set aside for incoming brides or are hosted by one of the prominent families.

My sister and I have set up a rough campsite out near one of the mining pits and spend our days digging for gemstone. It's plentiful near the surface, and Queen Hope thinks exchanging gemstone for a trade ship is a spiffy idea. Our new home world is growing by leaps and bounds. We need not only more women for the multitude of unmated warriors but also supplies to outfit their new homes.

Kendra and I have signed contracts that we'll eventually take Draconian mates and settle here, so the sky's the limit. Truth be told, we do plan to live here, right after we make one final trip to Earth. Though that's not part of the approved plan, I'll bet if we return with extra female settlers, the new provisional government will be happy as clams. Since Earth is slowly dying, I'm certain we'll have more volunteers than space to haul them. I just need to stick to my plan.

Tabor's normally blank expression was scrunched into a frown as he looked at Kendra. It's pretty clear that he doesn't think she should be looking at the younger warriors and I can guess why. We're the dirty scruffy outsiders, even on this out-of-the-way planet. No one's ever wanted us around, and these warriors are no different. Screw them all!

I also know why Kendra is staring at the young males. It's because there are so few guys her age to choose from. If she doesn't want to end up with someone twice her age, those are two of the maybe dozen on the planet. Since there are new women coming all the time, and often with children and teens, she has a small window of opportunity to lure a mate. Normally, I'd say she's too young, but the situation is what it is.

I know that I need to do something to help her be more appealing to the few young warriors she meets, but the truth is we don't have time to waste on mating right now, much less uptight warriors like Tabor or worrying about why no men are interested in mating with us. Time is of the essence.

That's why we're leaving for Denar Five shortly. It's the first step in my plan and the closest planet where I can find a used ship and enough spare parts to get it running. Kendra and I spent every waking moment learning ship repairs during our trip to this planet. Granted, we both worked as mechanics on Earth, but since everything went to crap, there wasn't much work about. That's why we signed up for the bride's registry, to get off planet and try to scare up resources to go back for the ones we left behind. None of the jobs we did on Earth would have prepared us to work on a spaceship anyways. We had to learn that in real time while getting attacked by the Moltan. Thank God we made it out of that skirmish alive.

Squeezing my sister's shoulder, I decide to do what I can for her. "Come on Kendra, we need to talk."

Her hear swivels around and her eyes lock with mine. "What's up? Am I in trouble again?"

Grinning like a mad fool, I shake my head. "Not this time. Let's get out of here and I'll tell you all about it."

Coming swiftly to her feet, she follows me out a side door and outside the training dojo. I pull her down onto a nearby bench and we huddle close. "We need to talk about finding you a husband."

Her eyes dart around. "I know we signed that contract but I don't want to end up with an old man. If it comes down to that, I'd rather die."

"Don't be so dramatic. It won't come down to that, because there are a dozen warriors in your age group to choose from. I realize that's a very limited selection..."

She whispers quickly, "There are only nine left. Three have been mated over the last few weeks. The good news is that there are only five women left under the age of twenty-five. That leaves me with four to choose from."

Taking her hands in mine, I try to keep some kindness in my voice rather than the cold fear that's in danger of edging in. "More ships are landing every day. We don't know how many are carrying younger women."

Her face falls and her eyes drift closed. "No one wants us. You know that. We both know that deep down inside."

"We just need to work on our image. I want you out of that uniform and at least in clean clothing. I know we've been frantic to scrape together enough gemstone to get us back home, but we can't keep running around with dirt on our clothing and sweaty faces."

"We're working twenty-hour days, grabbing a shower and food, and hopping back down into the pit. I don't think it makes much sense to doll ourselves up between bouts of hard manual labor."

The truth of her words sucks all the motivation right out of me. When I open my mouth, no words come out, so I snap it shut again.

Her voice sounds guilty. "What about you? Do you plan to make sure you're looking hot when we're around men?"

Suddenly, I see the humor in our sad little situation and snort a laugh. "I've got plenty of warriors to pick from, so there's no rush. Maybe there's one out there that likes dirty little ragamuffins like me."

Grinning back at me, she quips, "Well, I hope he has a brother."

I suck in a deep breath and try again. "All right, we'll make a pact. Once we leave this planet, we'll wear uniforms for work and clean up real nice when we're off duty." I hold out my hand for her to shake.

Tentatively putting her hand in mine, she chews her bottom lip.

"What are you thinking?" I can't imagine how difficult this situation is for her.

"You signed on one of the young warriors to our crew."

Nodding, I murmur, "He's a fully trained healer. We need his skills. Is he the one you were staring at? He's pretty handsome."

Shrugging, she replies casually, "I was just checking them both out."

"Tabor recommended the other one and he signed on as a scout. They say he's good at tracking down parts and people. I figured that since he's small, he might fit in tight spaces and be able to reach things the larger warriors can't when we're tearing parts out of old vehicles at the shipyard."

As she draws her hand back from shaking mine, she looks pensive. "Correct me if I'm wrong, but neither of them can get chosen by another queen if they're on this mission with us."

I see where her mind is. "You're absolutely right. I like where your head is on this one. Want me to see if we can sign a few more of the younger ones onto our crew?"

"Nope. I've got plans for those two."

I jolt upright in my seat. "You can't have two mates. That would be greedy."

"I never said that I wanted both of them."

Suddenly, it hits me what her plan is, and I give her a stern warning. "You're playing with fire, and if you're not real careful you will get burnt, sis."

Giving me a snazzy two finger salute, she deadpans back, "Your concerns are duly noted, Queen Kearney."

"Don't call me that. You know how much I hate it."

Kendra leans back and stretches her arms above her head, yawning. "Speak for yourself. I'm looking forward to being treated like royalty by my guy. Are you up for one more trek through the gemstone pit?"

I stand and stretch too. "Sure, why not. Everything in the 'verse seems to cost a fortune. We're lucky that we can just dig up gemstones to pay our way. Do you want to stop and get some food to take with us for tonight?"

"Hell no, until we make our final run to Earth, I'll drink hydration packs and eat food bars."

I can't help but smile. Kendra is about as self-sacrificing as I am. Nothing comes before our final trip. We both pick up our speed. Time is money, literally in our case.

On our way back, I can't help but feel a little happier. Just knowing that Kendra might have a chance at a real relationship warms my soul. I decide to have words with Tabor when he next crosses my path. I won't have him interfering in her personal life.

Images of my parents drift through my mind. Her meeting him at the door when he came home. The two of them cuddled on the sofa, kissing and holding hands. I can still remember the way he smiled at her. He always had a big sappy look on his face when they were together. That's the image burned into my mind about love, not the blank expressions all the warriors wear when they look at my grubby clothing and dirty skin.

I remember the devastated expression Mama wore after our father passed, and how we were her only solace and source of happiness for the last few months before we left Earth. Even though she was grieving, she always made us all feel wanted and loved. Emotion swells in my chest, threatening to close off my throat. I know deep down inside that I'm not half the woman my mother is. Yet, she's stuck, starving on Earth, and I'm here wallowing in gemstone.

We've got to get back to her before it's too late. I imagine what's left of our little family, huddled in a cave, slowly going through their rations. Kendra and I bought them a provision from the money we got after signing up for the bride's registry. It was a substantial amount, but food is expensive on Earth, and there were many mouths to feed. I've ordered several crates of food bars to take with us because I want them to have the nutrient-dense ones when we first arrive. Knowing they are probably starving is why my sister and I would burn in hell before we enjoyed a nice meal while our loved ones waste away, shivering in the cold.

After we got our payout, we huddled and went through all our options. Even with our combined payouts, we couldn't afford to house them in one of the huge underground cities. That left two options. They could be homeless in the lower level, which was riddled with crime and drugs or they could be renegades. Renegades were few and far between. They lived in underground bunkers or deep dark caves. Since we knew of a huge underground cave from before the fall, my family elected to go there.

Kendra and I made trip after trip with warm blankets, tarps for the ground to keep the moisture out of their bedding. We bought cases of food pellets, oatmeal, wheat and dehydrated foodstuffs. We searched out any cheap food we could find and a water purification unit for the strange stagnant water that ran through the back of the cave. We spent another several weeks gathering firewood and hauling large logs to bank down their fires. Lastly we secured one course of antibiotics in case one of them became ill. It was all we could afford. Looking back, that was almost two years ago and seems like far too little to sustain their numbers.

ister Queens

~ Tabor ~

The shuttle jolts beneath our feet. Since there is standing room only, we are each holding onto a safety ring situated overhead. It's almost comical how we all jerk forward at the same time, like puppets controlled by the same master. Phan glances back at me. Though he's proficient at maintaining a warrior's face, I can see the amusement in his eyes. Suddenly, the shuttle stabilizes and the back and side doors pop open and slide straight up, revealing the stark arid desert of Denar Five.

We chose this destination because it is a junkyard planet, and we have but one task. We are to build a ship worthy of a queen, or in our case two queens. The sister queens, Kearney and Kendra have determined they wish to be traders and have called forth about fifty warriors to crew their ship. My brother and I decided to strike out on our own. The humdrum activity of residing on our new home world seems dull compared to excitement of being in space. We now have queens to serve and protect, which give us a feeling of direction and pride.

Disembarking, we wait for the other two shuttles to land. Queen Hope's ship brought us to this planet. However the Raspian is sorely needed to stand sentry around our home world and perform other necessary missions. Therefore, it will stay in orbit only long enough to drop us off and for their shuttles to return.

We all snap to attention when the sister queens step from their shuttle. I've never seen two queens who looked more alike than Queen Kearney and Queen Kendra. Both of the fair skinned females have very long pale-yellow hair, which they normally keep pulled back off their faces in a long cascade down their back. Wary light blue eyes dart around anxiously, scanning for danger. I have often thought they must have had unpleasant experiences with males to be so hypervigilant.

I commanded their ship briefly when we rescued them from attack by the Moltan. They no longer look frail, dirty and gaunt like they did when we first met them. Though still too thin for my liking, they've filled out somewhat.

My mouth dries as my eyes slide over the older one's gently rounded hips. She's wearing a tight-fitting flight suit. Though her waist is tiny, the magnetic seams appear to be about to burst apart at the chest and again across her hips. She is wearing a uniform designed for a male youth—and it shows. If the seams did indeed burst, one can only imagine what delights would spill forth.

Phan's wings rustle slightly, and I notice that he's staring at the younger queen again. More than staring, I think. Warriors never miss an opportunity to gaze upon a queen, but my brother's preoccupation with Queen Kendra is concerning and obvious. I hate to see him take such an interest in her, when it's clear she is preoccupied with Timric. It must be confusing for my brother, because he is always standing side by side with his friend. My brother has barely earned his first stripe and dares to wish for a queen of his own already. His ambition would be shocking if it weren't born of such innocence.

I state quietly, "You make yourself obvious, brother. Guard your eyes."

Not looking at me, he continues to stare at the young queen. "Why should I? I am as worthy as any warrior to be chosen."

Timric glances from one to the other of us and keeps his head down. Smart young warrior that he is, Timric clearly is not ready to be chosen.

It's exasperating that Phan sees all others around us being chosen, and it leads him to think that luring a queen is easy. If he bothered to simply do the math, he'd know that our chances of being chosen are astronomical. Our clade is neither prominent, nor are we actual breeders. We are warriors with pretty faces and nice bodies that queens use for pleasure before casting us aside in favor of true breeders. I have seen it happen often. Our sire was humiliated to be cast aside. I have no desire to grow a genuine liking for a queen, only to fall out of favor and be forced to stand by while she bestows her affection upon a male capable of producing many young in one breeding cycle. Why would any queen settle for a male who can only spawn only one or two hatchlings, while there are males who can spawn a dozen at a time?

It is a moot issue since these queens in particular do not seem inclined to mate. Their beds are always bare of warriors. I've never known queens who did not allow warriors to tend to their needs. Perhaps they are born of a clad that has no such needs to tend.

The queens move forward in unison, their eyes seeking out their commander. Tearing myself from my internal musings, I step forward to meet them. Dropping onto one knee, I touch the ground with one hand. It is the traditional posture of submission, and it bothers me not to take it, because I know they are trustworthy queens.

"Rise, Tabor, and give your report." Queen Kearney's voice holds a note of resignation, and I decide this mission is important to her. I will endeavor to do my best to ensure she is not disappointed.

I come to my feet and heft my wing base up into the correct position for walking, rather than flying. "Welcome to Denar Five, my queens." The other males move around us, unloading the cargo I've carefully packed for this mission. "I've selected eight ships for you to inspect. Five are freighters, one is a battle cruiser, and the other two are mid-size trade vessels."

"Are the Denarians agreeable to us making repairs on their planet? I remember there being some objection to that during the negotiations, and I'm not wild about hauling all this junk into space to put it together."

"We worked that out by offering a substantial bonus. Your quarters should be set up within about thirty microns. Would you like to refresh yourselves before inspecting the wares?"

Queen Kendra chimed in, "Heck, no. We've been sitting around for days. I've been bored out of my mind. We should get right to work."

Her older sister queen nods her head in agreement. "Let's not waste any time. I want to get a ship up and running as soon as possible."

I can't help but wonder what the rush is, but I remain silent. Questioning the motivation of queens is taboo among my kind. I also have no wish to displease a queen simply to satisfy my own curiosity. Queens are wise and competent leaders. Mine has done nothing to suggest she is anything other than eager to get the job done.

"If you will follow me, we will speak with the owners of this stockyard, and then we will seek out the perfect ship for your needs. I have mapped where the most desirable vessels are located."

When I turn, they come up on each side of me. The guards I've assigned fall into line behind us. Naturally, Phan and Timric are not on the roster of guards I assigned to watch over our queens.

The sister queens are eager to see everything and meet the

beings who run the business. Denarians are huge creatures with thick muscular tentacle arms and legs. A round sheath of leathery skin covers their head, and four shoulders ending in eight long, tentacle-shaped arms. Another sheath of thick skin juts out from under their arms going down to form six thick, tentacle-like legs. The creature has no suckers on the underside of their arms and legs like some species. The have thick ridges that make picking up spare parts easy. They don't speak or make any kind of noise that a humanoid can discern. All their communication takes place through electronic devices. Each Denarian carries a huge electronic tablet the size of a sleeping platform, slipping it into a specially designed case on the creature's back when not in use. In turn, we stand at one of the dozens of communication terminals to key in our request. It's really just a metal podium jutting out of the sand with a generously sized tablet mounted to the top. Simple power rods power each station. I can see them clearly, running up the front of each podium.

When Kearney approaches the podium, one of the creatures drops to the ground beside her. The creature yanks out its tablet from its backpack and flops the tablet onto the ground beside her too. The ground trembles when the tablet hits the ground, causing junk to shift in a nearby pile.

My hand moves to my weapon when the creature leans over and runs one gigantic eye up and down our queen. Its eye is actually larger than the slight human queen. Though Denarians have a long history of nonviolence in this sector, I don't like him eyeing her that way. Suddenly, he pulls back and begins pounding on his tablet with one thick tentacle. Our queen responds to his greeting using the smaller device they've provided for us.

My wings tremble and I allow them to quietly unfurl in case there is a need to whisk her away. She glances back at me with anxiety in her eyes. Every protective instinct surges to the forefront of my consciousness, and I step closer. They negotiate back and forth. He wants something from her that she does not want to give, but I can't make out what it is. I can't read their conversation and keep an eye out for danger.

She pounds angrily upon the keys of the ancient communication device, cursing softly under her breath. The younger queen speaks, "Just say yes. It's no big deal."

In that moment I realize she's been standing on the other side of Queen Kearney this whole time and I didn't know it. "I don't like it."

"It's just hair. They're offering you a thirty-eight percent discount on every single thing you purchase. That's a fantastic deal for hair. It'll grow back."

"I guess you're right."

She spends several more minutes keying in information. Then a green holographic disk forms in the air above the tablet. It's her biometric seal. The creature has one too. We all do, because without a biometric seal, one cannot conduct business transactions in this sector of space. Their seals rise and begin drifting towards one another, his growing smaller to match hers in size. They merge into a transaction stamp, and I record it for verification of the deal they struck.

Windows open up in the Denarian's office building and drones come flying out. They are worker bots, but I can't imagine what they will do.

Queen Kearney steps back and puts her arms down to her side. "Take mine first and remember to leave exactly the amount we agreed upon."

The bots descend upon her and begin clipping sections of her hair and flying away with them. Within moments her long hair is no more. The bots have left just enough to cover her shoulders. Turning to her younger sister, she reassures her, "It doesn't hurt. It actually kind of tickles. Sorry about this."

Shrugging, the younger queen steps back with her arms down and takes the same exact pose her sister did. "Less hair to deal with, I guess." The bots come back, snipping her hair away as well. Now they look more like twins than ever, yet I am somehow sick to my stomach. It feels like something of value has been stripped from them. I quell my anger, for it is as Queen Kendra has said, it will grow back. Many queens wear their hair shorter, therefore all is well.

The creature retreats back into its cavernous hole and the queens both lean on each other, laughing and talking about how weird that was. They are not bothered, so why am I?

Where most queens are aloof and give off an aura of superiority, these queens appear to be excited and engaged. I remember that they've spent their lives on Earth before knowing only the inside of ships. My heart softens towards them and I see them in a different light. They are clearly enchanted by all the new sights and sounds.

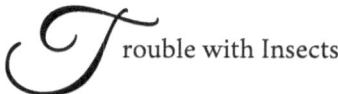 rouble with Insects

~ Kearney ~

Excitement strums through my chest. I can hardly believe we're actually here. Why that Denarian was so focused on having our hair is a mystery, but giving it up will save us a gigantic chunk off our final purchase. It feels kind of nice to be rid of it. I feel lighter and cleaner. Okay, that cleaner doesn't make any sense, but whatever.

All our hard work these past months in the gemstone mine really paid off. With any luck, we'll find a ship and have enough credits and mechanics in our midst to get it running fairly soon. After trading our gemstone for universal spending credits, I'm carefully managing our credit account to ensure we can complete this mission. Hopefully I've accounted for every expense.

The warriors who've signed onto our crew were used to working for free before being liberated, so waiting to get paid is no big deal for them. We laid in food stocks and other provisions to last for three lunars. I'm praying that will be enough time to get a ship up and running. Everything is riding on this mission.

"Kendra, don't touch that!" Seeing her reaching out to touch the sharp points on a nearby cactus-like bush worries me. She pulls her hand back just as the bush moves towards her. One of the warriors pulls her back out of its reach.

She shoots me a wide-eyed look, mouthing sorry. She's seventeen now, but still so inquisitive about alien worlds. I point to the ground at my side and she shuffles over to walk beside me, clearly embarrassed by her latest brush with death. Okay, that might be a little dramatic, but one never quite knows how dangerous the prick of an alien plant might be to a human. We only have the most rudimentary medical instruments with us, so we can't afford to take any chances.

Tabor stands aside and we stare straight up at the most amazing ship I've ever seen. It's a dull gunmetal grey but huge. It must have been here for a while because it's buried in the sand up to the manifolds. Shielding my eyes with one hand, I give it the once-over.

"What's the story on this one, Tabor?"

Reading from his data pad, he explains, "The Bellanthrop was engineered by the Denarians approximately seven hundred Earth years ago, to fight in the civil war that ended up killing over forty percent of their people. It was modified by a group of Strovian traders. Since they are humanoid, their renovations should have involved modification of the internal life supports to be more in line with our needs. None of the weapons systems were upgraded, so we can simply clear out munitions sections and retrofit them to accommodate our weapons."

Curiosity is getting the better of me. "Can we have a look inside?"

Our accommodating commander responds immediately. "Certainly, I'll open the main hatch."

Before I can respond, he turns, and with a quick jump, his wings unfurl, and he takes flight. I motion for one of the other warriors to follow him. The logical side of my brain is telling me there is likely no danger in him entering an old ship, but something in my gut is squirming again. I don't want to take any chances on a negative outcome. I need Tabor's expertise on this mission.

The waiting seems to last longer than I'm expecting. Pacing, I start to worry in earnest.

Kendra speaks up. "Should we send in another warrior?"

I jerk my chin at the one remaining warrior, and he lifts off. Do I feel uncomfortable on an alien planet without a protector? You bet I do. However, I feel even more uncomfortable about our commander taking so long to open the freaking door.

Something creeps up to Kendra, and she absent-mindedly pats it on the head. I don't know exactly what the creature is, but it looks like a cross between a lizard and a dog. Except for the horns and sharp teeth, it looks harmless. I take a step closer, and it jumps back. The next thing I know, it plops down on its bottom and scratches behind its horn with one of its six paws.

Before I can decide if the creature is male or female, a loud irritating screeching noise sounds off. Excitement strums though my chest when I realize the sound is coming from the ship.

Bolting forward, my sister exclaims loudly, "They did it! The door is opening."

She ain't wrong. A huge swath of slightly different-colored metal is slowly swinging down. The door is long, and it reminds me of the huge bay doors on some of the ships we've seen. The three men come flying out and touch down on the ground about fifteen feet from us. When we begin walking towards each other, I notice Tabor's got some kind of slash down the side of his face. It makes him look even more fierce than usual. My girl parts throb, but I push those thoughts away, intent on keeping it all business.

Feeling a frown crease my brow, I ask worriedly, "What happened in there?"

"Flying insects swarmed me. We'll need to scan the ship and eliminate them before you can inspect the interior."

"Let's head back to camp and make sure their stings aren't poisonous. We can pick back up with this later."

He shoots me a confused look. "I'm fine, but we've only got an hour or so of daylight left."

Crossing my arms, I stare him down. "We're going back. I'm not taking any chances on losing warriors over easily preventable issues."

He snorts a laugh before he thinks, and then his expression turns mortified. "It will be as you say, my queen."

I roll my eyes. Maybe I'm being over cautious, but most things that sting have venom. He might feel fine now, but later it could get into his bloodstream and kill him. As we walk the several hundred feet back to the makeshift camp the others have created, I quiz him about the ship.

"Did it seem spacious inside?"

"Absolutely. The Strovian upgrades are more well-preserved than I would have expected. I suppose the arid climate is responsible for our good fortune."

"Would it be strange if we ended up picking the very first one we inspected?"

"Not really. I chose the best of the lot for you to see first. It's the only one with a back-up propulsion system. That would be a real advantage if our primary system bot knocked out during a battle. It will be very few…."

His voice gets choppy, and I notice that he's sweating profusely. I pull my water canister from my waist pouch and grab a white scarf from my belt. Without taking my eyes off the commander, I shout my sister's name.

"I'm on it." The sound of her talking into her communicator is drowned out by Tabor continuing to talk about the interior of the ship. "entire bottom of the ship is one gigantic cargo bay. We could…fit…a lot…"

I step to his side just as he starts to go down and lower him safely to the ground. After dumping some water onto my scarf, I begin to wipe away the blood from his starkly masculine face. The horns that are normally standing straight up are now slicked back against his head. Though he's got no hair, he has some kind of intricate design inked into his flesh. "Tabor, let me wet your lips. You can't drink until we figure out what's going on with your injury." His eyes are glassy, and I'm shocked at how quickly the huge warrior went from making perfect sense to being nonsensical.

I pour some water into the palm of my hand and dump it onto his forehead, running my wet fingers down to moisten his lips. He grabs my hand unexpectedly. "Chose Drag for your next commander." Seeming to wilt before my very eyes, he rasps, "He'll keep you safe."

Oh God, he thinks he's going to die. Swallowing thickly, I wonder where the medical team is. The two remaining warriors are walking some kind of perimeter around us with their weapons out. It's clear from the upwards orientation of their weapons that they're protecting us from the flying insects.

Kendra shouts, "Over here. Quick. The commander is sick."

Several warriors alight on the ground nearby, and one is carrying a hover board. They move Tabor onto it, and the warrior attending to him seems too young to be a healer. He gently brushes past me, hooking up monitors and throwing up hovering equipment. He runs a metal sensor down the ugly cut on the commander's face and frowns.

I explain, "He went into one of the ships and got stung by an insect."

One of the other males speaks up. "They were each the size of my head and very aggressive."

The young healer responds tersely. "I couldn't pick up enough venom to engineer a proper antidote."

I turn to the two warriors who've been inside the ship. "Go back in. Take as many warriors as you need and bring back one of the insects as quickly as possible."

They jump into the air and head back to the large opening with several more warriors at their back.

The young medic seems agitated. He bends his head until he is touching foreheads with the commander, and I hear him whisper. "Don't worry brother. Everything's going to be okay." Something about his behavior is off. Draconian warriors often call themselves brothers, but they don't touch foreheads. Something tells me the healer is his actual brother or some other close relative. He pulls back, fiddles with his medical instruments. The time seems to drag by. Suddenly, the commander's body jerks violently. Before I can even blink, the medic lays a long, thin, black strip down the front of his brother's body and activates a stasis field.

He falls back onto his ass, resting one arm on his knee. He seems shell-shocked and sick to his stomach. "I should have come with him."

I reach out and touch his hand. "If you had gone into the ship, we wouldn't have a medic to mix the antivenom."

"We need to get him back to camp. I have more equipment there."

I motion to the several warriors still milling about to move him. All but one takes to the air. I guess they've decided the insects prefer the dark ships to the sunlight. That's the decision I've come to anyway.

One look at Kendra and I know exactly what she's thinking.

Flinging out her hands in an exasperated gesture, she shouts, "How did things go so wrong so freaking fast?"

We begin running back to our campsite. "I don't know, but we need to get back right damn now. Just as we come to a skidding stop into the campsite, the other warriors land with a big fat ugly insect. It's so large the man carrying it can barely get his fingers closed around its dead neck.

There is only one tent, and we head for it. I recognize that it's been set up for us but the medic has had his brother in an open-air lean-to along the side of our tent.

31

I walk up to him and place my hand on his shoulder. His head jerks around and he instinctively apologizes. "Sorry about violating your space…"

"Bring him inside along with your equipment."

Within moments they are pulling the hover board into our tent. I quickly pull back the blankets on our bed and motion for them to bring him over. "It's getting cold. I don't want him fighting the cold while you're working on him."

"Thank you my queen. Our clade owes you a debt of gratitude."

"Don't mention it. What else can we do to help?"

Before he can answer, other men pitch in and begin pulling medical supplies from the crates and setting up what begins to look like a small infirmary. Looking over my shoulder, I see Kendra sitting on her bed with her legs crossed. She's staring at the healer as he works. Her face is contorted into a mask of anxiety. Like me, she's feeling useless. All we can do is stay out of the way, so I cross the space, climb on the bed and drape my arm around her shoulder. Without tearing her eyes away from the commander, she pats my hand. "He's going to make it, right?"

Since I can't imagine pulling off this mission without him, I lie my ass off. "Of course he's going to be okay."

ugs Out

~ Tabor ~

I wake feeling like absolute garbage. The entire right side of my body feels like insects are crawling on my skin and my fingers are on fire. The last thing I remember is my father's face growing smaller in my view screen as I lift off from our home world. I try to clear my head by shaking it. A cool cloth smooths over the side of my face, and small soft hands moisten my lips with water.

Queen Kearney's face finally comes into focus. "Are you really awake this time?"

"I am." My voice is dry, and I sound like a swallowed a small creature.

Phan's face comes into view, and I realize that I'm lying down staring up at them.

"How do you feel, my brother?" His worried expression makes me feel valued.

"My right arm tingles."

He pulls out a medical scanner and begins moving it back and forth. "It is the nanobots repairing your injured blood vessels. The inset's venom got into your blood stream and began eating through the walls of your blood vessels. Do not worry, it should dissipate soon." His concerned expression is still in place as he continues to scan my right side.

"My fingers feel like they're on fire."

Jerking slightly, his eyes jump to mine. "I can fix that." His face disappears. The next thing I know, a hypodermic spray touches my neck, and all I see is blackness.

When next I wake, our queen is still tending to my needs. She looks exhausted, and it makes me wonder how long I have been down. I raise my hand to grasp hers, and she stops smoothing the cool wet cloth over my face.

Her eyes are worried. "Phan says all the damage to your system has been healed. You just need to gather your strength again."

"How about you? Are you well, my queen?"

Swallowing thickly, she glances across the room. When my eyes follow hers, I see my brother on the same sleeping platform as the young queen. Closing my eyes, I tell myself he is not being chosen. He's exhausted from performing his medical duties, and resting nearby affords him the opportunity to check on me.

"How long have I been out?"

"Two days. How do you feel? Can you sit up and drink some broth?"

Struggling to sit, I manage it by sheer willpower alone. I am ravenous and grateful when she brings a warm cup of vegetable broth to my lips. She gently encourages me to drink my fill before speaking again.

"I put Drag in charge of the other warriors like you asked. He seemed a little unsure of himself at times, so I asked one of the elders to assist him. I believe his name is Elder Scarn. He's really nice."

I lean back against the cushions she's stuffing behind me, cushions I chose with care to ensure the queens rested comfortably. "Did you choose a ship yet?"

Adjusting a cushion roughly behind my shoulder, she sighs.

"I looked over the list of vessels you sent me. We had a hard time figuring out the pros and cons of each, so I had them begin scavenging parts for the medical bay, hydroponics bay and cluster B weapons arrays."

"That's smart, because all those systems are fairly standard across different ships."

"Are you really feeling better?"

"Yes."

"We were worried about you." Her eyes hold an element of warmth, but her expression is still guarded.

"I'm fine. Do you want to go over the ships I selected? I can give you the rundown on each design."

"Sure." Sitting gingerly on the side of the sleeping platform, she pulls out her electronic tablet.

When she pulls up the first design, I begin explaining what I like about it. "It's been renovated once already. The work was high quality, and we can modify it more quickly than the other ships they have for sale. It's designed to carry backup fuel rods so we can go longer between fuel stops."

"I noticed the entire bottom layer is one gigantic cargo bay that can be accessed from either side of the ship. You actually mentioned that one before you were poisoned."

I swallow thickly. I'm certain that getting myself taken out by a flying insect before the mission even got off the ground makes me look pretty weak and foolish in her eyes. Up close, I can tell those eyes are beautiful, as is her pale hair. Resisting the urge to reach out and touch her soft strands, I speak to what's bearing on my mind. "I suppose you will continue with Drag as your commander, since I made such a poor showing at the beginning of this mission."

Her carefully schooled expression slips and I can see her

surprise. "Once you are feeling rested, I would prefer that you take up your duties."

"You do not think me incompetent?"

Reaching behind me to adjust my cushions, she murmurs, "We're just grateful that you pulled through."

Her scent is delicate and feminine, and she still wants me to lead her mission. Invigorated, I ask crisply, "Would you like to hear about the other ships?"

She nods and scoots closer to look at the data on the tablet. I had them send aerial drones in to capture images from the interiors of the rest of the ships. The five freighters were severely damaged on the inside, three were rusted beyond repair."

"Those would have been my first choice because they eat fuel rods. What did the others look like?"

"They were in varying stages of deterioration. I don't know enough about ships to know which ones could be salvaged. I sent you the video footage we captured. Have a look for yourself."

I click open each file and we watch the footage together. Being so near a queen affects me more than I imagined it would. Thrilled when she inches closer, I force myself to focus on the images. If I don't pay attention, I won't be able to have a coherent dialogue.

"Thought the battle cruisers are fast and have exterior mountings for phase cannons, I believe they lack the cargo room of the mid-range bulk transports."

"I suppose if we're down to the two mid-range transports the one with the retrofits is the better option. Do you have any ideas on how to clear the insects out?"

Feeling a surge of energy, I sit upright. When I pull back the blanket, I can see they've taken off my uniform, and I'm wearing only the long undergarments that cling to my legs. The top hangs low on my waist and when I stand, Queen Kearney's eyes travel down my body like she's assessing my ability to breed. Whatever she was looking for, she clearly does not find, because she jerks backward and whirls around groping for something on a nearby table.

She holds out a fresh uniform and I grab it, covering my offending body as quickly as possible. The movement wakes Phan who flies from his sleeping mat to check on me. His scanner is in his hand and moving over me before I can object. "It looks like you are fully recovered. There is no trace of the venom in your body and the nanobots have deactivated, which means there were no more repairs to be made. How do you feel?"

Catching a glimpse of our queen over his shoulder, I respond tightly, "I feel like I could fly circles around the moon."

"I'm not surprised. I pumped you full of healing serum once the nanobots began to slow down."

It's the energy boost we give our young warriors when they first begin to train in earnest. It helps them bulk up and keeps them healthy while they put their young bodies through the rigors of training to be a warrior. I give his shoulder a quick squeeze. "Thanks, brother. Do you want to help me clear the insects out of our queen's new ship?"

His face lights up, reminding me how much my brother enjoys action and adventure. "You know I do. I'm eager to learn a little more about their biology and breeding habits. Discovering a new species is always intriguing."

"The suns will be up within the hour. I was foolish to go in without wearing armored battle gear. We won't make that mistake this time."

"I'll wake the others, sir."

Bowing our heads slightly, we murmur respectful farewells to our queen. I step outside her tent and haul in a deep gulp of the cool, early-morning air before heading over to the barracks. It consists of a thick tarp on the ground and a sturdy open-air canopy meant to keep the rain off the warriors while they sleep. Of course on this arid planet, the canopy seems like a waste of time. We gear up and make ready to swarm the ship in full force. After being on my back for two days, I'm aching to do something physical.

Leaving only a handful of warriors guarding our queens, we head to the ship. Phan and his battle buddy have not stopped whispering since we hit the makeshift barracks. Granted, they're always putting their heads together about something, but they seem more excited than usual. It makes me wonder if the young queen initiated courting rituals with him.

I activate my face shield as we near the vessel. Since we've never encountered this particular species of insects before, and Drag reported that the locals insist they've never seen anything like it, it is likely they were already nesting on the ship when it was sold. If so, they've been festering there for three solars. I will need to activate the ship's internal scans to make sure we eradicate every single insect in order for the queens to be safe aboard this vessel.

We move forward and step into the darkened interior. Several warriors release hovering mechanical devices to light our way. We make our way to an auxiliary substation, and two warriors begin working on a back-up power relay. They shove small emergency power rods into place, and the room lights up. We will have to do this in every section as we work our way to the engineering section of the ship.

Lifting my hand, I shout, "Hold."

The warriors all go still, and we hear a faint buzzing noise.

"Is that the insects?" Phan's voice is barely a whisper, but his eyes are huge.

I nod. "They came at me from the ceilings."

Half the warriors aim their weapons up, and the others continue to monitor the rest of the room. It's standard battle tactics.

Timric steps forward. "I'll scout ahead."

"Watch your back, warrior." He stalks off towards one door, and I motion for Elder Scarn and another to follow him. This is his first mission as a scout. Though I know Timric is ready, I will afford him backup for this mission.

Phan squats down and snaps images of a viscous white substance from the floor before scraping it up and carefully dropping it into a tiny stasis container. He runs it across the handheld device he used to capture images, leaving an imprint on the specimen box. My brother's compulsive attention to detail may yet win him an award among the healers. When he's finished, our unit moves cautiously forward.

We activate two more substations before getting a message from our scouts. They've discovered what appears to be a nest, with a queen, no less. Since a certain subset of insects breed using a primary queen, the news isn't all that shocking, I suppose. We meet resistance, and cut a path to our scouts using the pinpoint accuracy of our laser weapons.

When we burst into the dining area, Timric and Scarn are squatting with their laser rifles across their laps. Sprawled around are several insect bodies, and they are staring at the large queen. She almost the size of a warrior, and unlike the males of her species, she has three distinct segments. Since the males have two, I assume the last segment is for breeding. She's been webbed into place with what appears to be the sticky viscous substance Phan took a sample of when we first arrived. She looks pitiful and is making a keening noise. It's clear her drones have been force-breeding her.

My brother steps to my side, clearly shocked by what the insects have done to their queen. "How can any species treat their queen in such a way?"

"I do not know. Perhaps they are but mindless animals."

"She's an elder queen, and her breathing is labored. My initial reaction was to give her medical treatment, then I thought better of it."

We hear firing from the rear. "We're being attacked again. Euthanize their queen, and quickly gather whatever information you need on this species. We will cover you for as long as we can, but after that, we ensure none remain to infect our queens with their venom."

"Understood, sir." Phan unshoulders his medical kit and loads a hypo-spray. The queen cannot harm him in current circumstances, so I leave Scarn to watch over him and return to the fight. Darg fights shoulder to shoulder with me. "One thing is for certain, this species is as prolific as it is aggressive."

"This is a fact that I know all too well."

I shoot one as it is flying for my friend's back. It sends a clear message that we had better focus on the vicious swarm that's doing it's best to overwhelm our defenses.

aiting It Out

~ Kearney ~

Kendra can't seem to stop pacing. It's making me anxious as well. I've parked my carcass at a fold-up table and am scrolling through the footage from the battle with the insects that's still in progress. Nothing leads me to believe they are sentient beings. There is no strategy to their attack patterns, no cooperation with one another, and no attempts to communicate. The insects seem to be in a blind rage and have not quit swarming our warriors even now that it is clear their stingers cannot pierce the men's battle armor.

A worried voice sounds off behind me. "Why is it taking so long?"

Without looking up, I continue to monitor the footage. "The ship is large. They have to repair the sensors and then track down all the insect signatures. It's only been six hours. They might not be able get it all done in one day."

"They're going to break and come back here to sleep, right? I don't want them trying to bed down in there. It's too risky."

"It wouldn't make sense for them to stay there overnight. Have you eaten anything since this morning? You know how you get when you don't eat." I toss her a food bar, and she clutches it in her hand as she walks over to look out the doorway we made by pulling the flap of the tent back. "Staring out towards the ship isn't going to bring them back any faster."

"I want them out of harm's way. They're too young and inexperienced to be in such a dangerous situation."

All this time, I've been under the impression she's been worried about all our warriors. Now it sounds like she's more worried about the two younger warriors. "After spending a couple of days with Phan, I would have thought you might be well onto developing a friendship. However, you hardly know Meric's son. Why are you so worried about him?"

"Phan is pretty amazing, I'll admit that. Wouldn't it be cool if I ended up with him and you ended up with the commander?"

At almost eighteen, Kendra is still young enough to think that the two of us mating brothers would be awesome. Even I have to admit it would be convenient, not because they're brothers necessarily, more because they're good-looking, smart, capable, and seem really focused on us. Most warriors would burn in hell before they pursued a queen. It suddenly occurs to me that Tabor has done everything short of that.

He helped set up our campsite, made sure we had the tools and knowhow to dig for gemstone, and helped me sort and grade it. He traded out our food bars for some kind of super nutrient-dense ones that helps us pick up some weight, even while expending tremendous energy digging for gemstone every day. Tabor never judged. Instead he just helped and supported us, while looking ten kinds of handsome in the process.

I don't think even Kendra knows my deepest, darkest secret. Watching him fly makes my girl parts throb with need. Something about those huge wings flapping in the breeze flips all the right switches for me. Since he's very adept at reading my expressions, I'm careful never to look him in the face. If I did, he'd know for sure how I feel about him.

We can't have that when we're so close to making it back to Earth. I've got enough of those nutrient-dense food bars to feed my family for a very long time. We stocked huge crates of them, and you only need one a day to survive. Two a day makes life easy, because not only are there no hunger pains at the end of the day, but we were able to pick up weight. I wouldn't describe us as curvy, but I'm definitely getting there.

Rather than admit to anything, I murmur, "Sure, that would be nice. We need to get back to Earth before we begin any relationships, though. We talked about this, remember?"

"I don't see why we can't do both."

"Do what you want. I'm not wasting time on anything as long as we don't know what's going on with Mom."

"You're right. Sorry, I let myself get distracted."

I look up and catch her eye. "It's okay. At your age boys were all I thought about."

She gives me a knowing grin. "You must have been looking at them in a book, cause there were never enough boys to bother with on Earth."

She ain't wrong about that. On Earth almost fifty years ago a contagion born of pollution in Earth's oceans locked onto the male DNA. First the males began acting strange, flying off the handle and were easily irritated. Some began engaging in non-goal directed behaviors, like pinching at the air or rocking back and forth. It was difficult to tell something was wrong at first. Then emergency rooms were literally flooded with people reporting nonsensical symptoms. It took the medical community months to find the contagion and years to fabricate an inoculation. They never did manage to find a cure, costing millions of lives. The end result was by the time we were born there were very few males, especially in our age group.

Kendra dropped down onto a crate beside my makeshift table. "Do you think we should join them?"

"I think the commander's head would explode if we showed up without battle armor. I'm not keen on watching you go through the healing process if you get stung. The warriors are strong, and the commander is more robust than most of them. The poison almost killed him. It's not likely that you or I would survive being stung. We'd best let the warriors handle it, don't you think?"

Kendra wrinkles her nose in disgust. "I wish we had battle armor."

"It takes weeks to fabricate because its custom designed to the wearer's body. I wish we had it too, but I wasn't about to postpone our mission to get it."

"Do you think Mom and the others are getting by?" Her shaky voice tells me she already knows the answer to that question. She's wringing her hands in her lap just thinking about it.

"We left them in a cave with dehydrated food and only one course of antibiotics." Sighing heavily, I reach out and play one hand over hers. "We have to be prepared for the reality that some of them didn't make it."

My younger sister lifts her chin defiantly and her voice turns cold. "Kara's still alive. If she weren't, I'd know."

"I know why you think that, honestly I do. If anyone can survive, Kara can. She's always been in touch with nature in ways the rest of us weren't. She knows how to scavenge for berries and what mushrooms are safe to eat. She can start a fire without a fire starter and keep the coals going for days."

"I'm thinking that as far up in the mountains as they are, there's a chance she found a clean spring."

My throat closes up with emotion. "Before the fall, she always said it was coming. None of us believed her."

"They said we were just kids, and we didn't know what we were talking about."

I pull her into a bear hug. It's been a long time since Kendra spoke of them as a unit. It affects me more than I thought it would. "They'll be alive. We have to believe. If I begin doubting again, bring me up short."

Pulling back, Kendra has a sad smile on her face. "You better believe I will." Coming to her feet, she stretches. "Right now, I'm going to go out and work on that old shuttle with our guards."

My head jerks up to look at her. "Don't call them that. We aren't their prisoners."

"I know, I know. They work for us now. It just seems weird." She gives me her back and strolls out of the tent.

I go back to watching the data stream, paying particular attention to Tabor. He's a competent commander. All the men follow his order without hesitation. I zoom in on his face and am shocked that he's smiling. A quick look around tells me they all are, with the exception of Phan. I remember he's a healer, rather than a regular warrior so he probably doesn't enjoy a good fight as much as the others. Still, the young man holds his own, taking down as many insects as the others. My wariness of him turns to grudging admiration. He'd be a good catch for Kendra.

I notice his battle buddy sticks right by his side. Timric is his name. He's all warrior. I can tell because his fighting technique is similar to Tabor's, meaning he's super aggressive. He jumps forward to meet the enemy and doesn't hesitate to turn and jump over objects to get a good shot. He'd be a handful for some lucky lady, but not my sister. If that's Kendra's plan, we're going to butt heads.

I jolt up in my seat. They've arrived in the engineering section and appear to be working on the main engine. A small team leaves and returns about thirty microns later with large metal coil. I watch them retrofit it to the ship, cutting away about a third of it. I'm elated when the ship finally powers up. Our warriors are clever and hard-working men. The reward I have planned for them will make every bit of their diligence worth it.

They rig some kind of complicated grid of tubes and fiber optics they've pulled from various parts of the huge ship. They haven't cleared the entire ship of insects, so this makes we wonder if they're arranging for a radiation blast or something along those lines to kill the last of the insects. Tabor won't take a chance on anyone else being stung, that much is certain.

Suddenly, all the warriors take flight at the same time. I didn't know they could move that fast. Coming to my feet, I don't take my eyes off my data pad. At this point the warriors are moving faster than the floating cameras can keep up. I'm getting mostly images of the backs of the rapidly flapping wings. There is a blinding light and my data pad goes black.

Tossing it onto the table, I go running out of the tent. Kendra sees me running for the ship and joins me, with the other warriors at our heels.

"What happened?" She shouts in a rush as we run.

My heart is hammering, but I push out a breathless reply. "Something went wrong. There was a bright light and then everything went dark."

We skid to a stop in front of the huge ship and find the warriors lying and sitting on the ground. They begin getting up one by one, dusting off their uniforms. Without thinking, I run over to Tabor and fall to my knees beside him. "Are you all right? I saw the bright light and then everything went blank." My hands are running all over his chest and arms as I look for injuries.

"I am well, my queen."

The tone of his voice catches me off guard. He sounds surprised and somewhat amused by my little freak-out. I force myself to pull my hands off him and wrap them around my stomach, just so I'm not tempted to touch him again. "What happened?"

"We set off a scrubber. It's a burst of energy designed to eradicate all life, right down to microbes. We normally set it two microns behind a shield designed to keep us ahead of the eradication burst. In this case we were apparently not flying fast enough so it pushed us forcefully out the bay door. It was not enough pressure to cause injury, my queen."

"Good. I was just worried because you were just back from being down for a couple of days. So, the ship is bug free now?"

"Yes. We will spend the rest of the day clearing up the debris and then it will be safe for you and your sister queen to inspect."

"Well, that's good. Thank you."

"Are you well, my queen?"

A quick glance around tells me everyone is staring at us, or rather they're staring at me. I'm sure it looks like I'm fawning over Tabor. Sheesh. That is not what I intended. "Kendra and I will work on the shuttle today, and we'll all begin repairs on the ship tomorrow at first light. I want to be off this world as soon as possible."

Coming to his feet, Tabor extends his hand to help me up. "Understood, my queen. You will not find anyone dragging their wings on my watch."

ack of Trust

~ Tabor ~

Phan and Timric walk towards me, passing the queens with a respectful bow of their heads. Phan's eyes are huge and his wings pinned tightly back. "What in the 'verse was that all about, brother?"

I am shocked that our queen singled me out for attention and seemed so worried about my well-being. "Our queen has been through a large amount of stress over the last few lunars. After being attacked by the Moltan and seeing her commander injured, I believe she is wary of losing any of her warriors."

Phan lets out a deep breath. "She seems especially concerned about her commander."

I reply steadily, "Since I am the warrior she is most familiar with and have served her well, it stands to reason that she would wish to continue under my protection rather than having to familiarize herself with another commander."

Timric speaks up. "I believe the touching is common for queens when they wish to assess if a warrior is injured. Queen Stacy exhibited such behavior during my medical apprenticeship."

Swiveling his head around to look at his friend, Phan frowns. "Queen Stacy did this to my father before taking him to mate."

Timric replies thoughtfully. "Perhaps she was attempting to remove your uniform to look for injuries but did not know how."

Phan's voice drops slightly. "She wears a similar uniform herself. It stands to reason that she knows how to get it on and off."

"Yes, but your brother's uniform…"

"Enough. We have work to do and exactly no time for such useless banter. I want you both assisting the crew assigned to the bridge. They're going to need runners to hunt down parts in this area. Stay together and maintain an awareness of your surroundings."

My brother snaps to attention. "We will not fail you, commander. You may wish to inform the others that it is unlikely the insects we exterminated will be living out in the open. Their biology is made for low temperatures. I do not believe they could survive being exposed to the twin suns on this arid planet."

"I will send out a general message, but do not take any chances. Cover each other's back just the way you were trained."

They both acknowledge my command in unison and head back into the ship. I follow with Elder Scarn at my side. "It will take days to clear up all the debris, sir. The queens are eager to assist with the repairs. We clear out the loading bay first so we can store their cargo. I do not like our crates sitting out in the open unattended. Though there are few people about, our cargo will draw unwanted attention."

"That is a smart move. I believe we will wish to get the queens into a chamber where we can better protect them."

"They can sleep in the loading bay with the cargo."

Scarn's head whips around his wings unfurl. "Are you attempting to pick a fight with me, sir? You well know the loading bay is no fit place to house delicate human queens."

"The loading bay is enormous. I mean to simply move their luxurious tent, sleeping platforms and multitude of cushions into the bay temporarily until we can clear more of the ship."

Folding his wings back, Scarn responds sheepishly, "I don't know why I imagined them sleeping on the cold metal floor."

Giving his shoulder a squeeze, I give him a little shake. "I am an honorable warrior. Therefore, I will strive to make the sister queens as comfortable as possible while they shelter under my wing."

"They seem enamored with working on engines. Might I suggest we clear a path from the loading bay to engineering first? That will allow them to move between their private space and their favored worksite unencumbered."

"That is an excellent plan. I wish to get this ship operational and loaded with enough spare parts to ensure we can make repairs as needed."

"I notice you posted a list of parts we are to scavenge and it was weighty."

"This is an extremely resource-rich environment. I doubt we will find another salvage yard with such a diverse offering. Also, our queen has negotiated a deep discount on all that we buy."

"Why do you think the Denarians were so eager to make such a trade?"

"My best guess is they wish to trade them to one of the species who value cloning. Humans are lovely creatures. I can see an alien species wishing to mix human qualities with their own DNA. She struck a surprisingly good bargain with the Denarians. I'm inclined to pay at the discounted rate for spare parts now, rather than paying a premium for those same parts when we are in desperate need."

"You are wise beyond your years, commander. Not many see the benefit of planning so far into the future. Queen Kearney got the discount by trading their long hair.

"We are tasked with the safety with not just one precious queen, but two. The younger is barely of age to mate. It is my opinion that we cannot be too careful when it comes ensuring their health and wellbeing."

"Agreed. Shall I take a team to clear out the loading bay?"

"I will accompany you, Elder Scarn."

"The more hands the better, commander, but I thought your time would be better served on the bridge."

"My bridge crew is each seeing to his assigned area, so I will leave them to it. I'm not above clearing rubbish and am as strong as any warrior."

"Though few commanders are willing to perform menial labor, we are pleased to have you on our team today."

I flash him a grin as we enter the loading bay and we grab a huge piece of rusted metal and begin dragging it towards the bay door. The work is dirty and difficult, but I am pleased for the opportunity to flex my muscles.

For some reason, I continue to feel the effects of the warrior's serum my brother administered to aid me in my recovery. It makes the hard manual labor rather exhilarating but also provokes my thirst.

We pull off our tops after removing the bulk of the metal and begin repairing the bay doors, lighting, and environmentals. By dusk, my muscles ache a little from all the heavy lifting, but I am not tired. We stop and go out in the cool night air to suck down a hydration pack and eat our food bars. I've been living off food bars for so long, it doesn't occur to me to want real food. I only realize that's an option because the queens are planning everything they wish to grow in the hydroponics bay. It's confusing, because both sisters rejected all offerings of naturally grown foods on our home world. They insisted upon eating only food bars, which are nutrient dense but bland and tasteless.

Though it might considered rude to question the queens on their food preferences, I allow my curiosity to get the better of me. "Do you mind if I ask why you did not wish to eat from the dining hall during your time on our planet? Is it because you wish to consume only food that you have grown with your own hands?"

When Queen Kearney's eyes land on me, she seems taken aback. Instead of answering my question, her eyes skate over the wide expanse of my chest. Her gaze turns warm and admiring, and I wonder if she does think of me as a potential mate. Without meaning them to, my wings release a quarter of a turn and my muscles tighten. When her gaze drops down to my stomach muscles, my cock begins to harden.

I quickly shift my leg up to cover my crotch, and in doing so, deprive her of the sight of most of my body. I rest my arm casually on my knee and force myself to act normally. "If you wish, we can clear out the hydroponics bay and get your foodstuffs growing."

She jerks back and closes her eyes for a brief moment. "We were planning on picking up seeds on Earth."

All the warriors stop talking and turn to hear more about going to Earth. Since it is the one planet with excess unmated females, it is the place warriors most wish to visit. "I thought your plan was to trade with planets around our home world."

Lifting her chin, she replies sternly, "I never said that. I stated that I wish a trade ship and crew to conduct trade with other planets."

"The only item Earth has to trade is brides and the queens ruling our home world forbid us from purchasing or trading for human females."

"Am I not also a queen? Why should their wishes supersede mine?"

"There are many queens on our home world, but only two rule. We are obligated to follow their directives if we wish to remain on our world."

"I will visit Earth and trade my gemstone for seeds, cloth and other items human queens covet. When I return with these items they will be pleased. If they are angry, I'll look for another planet to call home."

"You should have selected more warriors if you wish to found a new world, my queen. We are fifty strong, but that is barely enough to staff your ship."

"Perhaps we will pick up extra crew from the many ports we stop at." Glancing around at the large group of warriors who are hanging on her every word, she raises her voice slightly. "I have heard many women on Earth wish to find jobs and earn their own way, rather than signing bride contracts. I'm certain many could learn basic ship functions."

Queen Kendra speaks as well. "They would be helpful in hydroponics and basic ship's maintenance. You don't have to have wings or be a genius to clean a fuel injector or replace a burned-out fuel rod."

The warriors all begin whispering to each other. Even I am excited at the thought of rescuing human queens from their dying world. I bow my head in submission, to the sister queens. It appears they have worked around the laws set down by our ruling queens. It is clear that where there are unmated queens, there is opportunity for our warriors to distinguish themselves. The warriors see this as an opportunity, as do I.

I glance at Elder Scarn, who dips his head in agreement. "So be it, Queen Kearney. All will be as you say."

She lets out a breath shakily and darts a look at her younger sister queen. The look that passes between them is one of slight relief, and then worry creases their brows. I also spy an emotion that appears to be a tinge of guilt, and it becomes clear to my mind that they have not been entirely truthful. Since I do not think that Queen Kearney would break the law outright or do anything to harm others, she must be holding back information because she does not find me trustworthy or thinks I am too ignorant to understand her plan.

Both of these possibilities truly wound my soul, for I have given of myself freely and bowed to their every whim. Looking away, I try to process the multitude of emotions threating to swamp me.

My chest is tight, and the ache is one I have never known. I feel rejected and humiliated before my brethren. But when I look around, I see they are too excited about visiting Earth to notice the slight. I rise to my feet and return to the ship. Since the queens' belongings have been arranged in the loading bay, I decide to work on the bridge. Being trained with a basic knowledge of repairing holographic imagers, I begin working on the large one that serves as the primary point of contact with other vessels.

I pull out all the filaments and sort through a pile Phan and Timric scavenged from other vessels. They are fresh and high quality, but designed for a shuttle. Therefore, I must couple them together to make them long enough to span the entire length of the imaging assembly. It is tedious work, but keeping busy helps take my mind off the apparently poor job I'm doing leading this mission. There is no getting around the fact that my queen has no trust in me.

I complete the repairs on the holographic imager and get to work on the smaller imagers at each console. My hands are occupied but my mind wanders. My battle buddy for many years was Meric. He not only captured the attention of a queen but ended up selected for mating. We are alike in all areas save one. He is a breeder with long golden hair, and I am a simple warrior. Queens prefer males who are excellent breeders, and I can only spawn two or maybe three young at a time. It is not Meric's being chosen where I was not that wounds my soul, it is not being seen worthy of my queen's trust.

 Ship of Our Own

~ Kearney ~

We're sweating because the environmentals are not functioning correctly yet, but I have to admit that I absolutely love this ship! Kendra and I have never had anything that was actually ours before, so we're totally stoked. Everyone seems enthusiastic about getting it up and running, and we're way ahead of schedule on the repairs. The only person who seems to be less than thrilled is Tabor.

Those eagle eyes of his don't miss much. He knew I wasn't telling the whole story last night. He doesn't know that I'm playing my cards close to the vest, telling them only what I think they need to know each step of the way. We couldn't very well set a trajectory for Earth without anyone noticing. So, I had to come clean about that piece. Nothing I said was a lie. I do intend to trade on Earth, right after I check on my family.

Truth be told, I didn't expect the crew to be so open to visiting Earth. In retrospect, it seems stupid not to put two and two together and realize guys looking for mates would want to visit a planet where they are plentiful. I guess that I had it in my mind that they were more interested in action and adventure or they would have stayed planet side where there is a whole building of women looking for mates. Then again, the odds were stacked against them. There is a good chance they thought that going from planet to planet would afford them more opportunities to meet alien females in general.

I wipe my hands on a cleaning cloth and head outside the ship. I can hear the warriors getting loud and am curious about what's going on. What I see makes me stop in my tracks. Kendra is with the two younger warriors. They're mixing what appears to be a large vat of metallic paint. It's copper colored and they seem to be having a blast. Kendra seems to have gotten close to them since we left. I see the strange dog-like creature she petted when we first arrived and it has her hand print in copper colored paint on his side. He's jumping around, making them laugh. Crew members are standing around and laughing at their shenanigans as well. The three of them are that strange age when they aren't kids anymore but aren't thought of as grown adults either.

The smile slips from my face, and I'm shocked at what I see next. She dips both hands in the paint and places a hand on each of their chests. This is a playful gesture, but one the crew will interpret as her selecting both of them for mating. Draconian warriors are big on marking their property, after all. They all create special designs and mark everything from their faces to their gear. They will call this her queen's mark. She marked the dog as her property and now the two males. Some women chose two men to mate, but not the women in our family. I know for a fact that's not what my sister is doing.

My eyes search around nervously for Tabor. I find him staring at them with an angry expression on his face. I'm a little confused. The Draconian are accustomed to sharing a queen, so why is he angry? The only thing I can figure is he thinks we're too scruffy for his brother, because we don't wear fancy clothing and demand pampering. We're atypical females.

Anger ignites hot and fast in my gut, but I swallow it back in favor of talking to him. There are so few age-mates for Kendra that I can't risk him messing this up for her. Stretching my neck sideways, I try to get rid of the cramp that's growing there. I begin walking towards him, but he spins on his heel and stalks back into the ship.

I pick up speed and follow as fast as my feet will carry me. I find him in an auxiliary relay junction. They are small nooks where a bunch of wires and pipes merge before branching off in different directions. "Are you angry about my sister leaving her mark on your brother?"

Without turning around he utters with a short clipped response. "It's not my place to judge the actions of a queen."

"You didn't look very happy for your brother. I thought all warriors wanted to be chosen."

"Again it does not matter what I think, so please stop asking. Queens speak and warriors obey. That is the natural order of things. If Queen Kendra wishes him, then it will be so."

"I know we don't always look or act like the way you expect queens should, but my sister is a good person. She'd never do anything to hurt Phan or embarrass him. You have to know that."

Finally turning to look at me, I can see the disappointment in his face. "I doubt she will spend enough time with him to do either."

My mouth falls open. "What do you mean by that?"

"Nothing," Turning away, he begins to work again.

I reach out and grab the top of his uniform that's now hanging about his waist. Trying to jerk him back proves to be a futile endeavor. I couldn't budge him if I wanted to. He's a mountain of muscle. "I demand that you tell me what your problem is this minute." His eyes find mine, and he can tell I'm not playing around.

He takes a minute to get his anger under control before speaking to me. "Our clad is full of warriors with pretty faces. We are accustomed to queens who choose us for sport before moving on to spawn with breeders. My own father was devastated to be cast aside. Even though the queens of old treated us horribly, to be chosen meant everything because it meant we could spawn and pass on our heritage. I wished better for my brother. That is all."

Instead of trying to return to his work, he tugs his clothing gently from my grip and melts back into the shadows. It takes me a minute to realize what he was attempting to communicate. Kendra marked Phan and his battle buddy, Timric, who's an actual breeder. Tabor thinks she's intent on using Phan for entertainment and Timric for breeding.

Hell, he doesn't know a damn thing about human women. Forget the fact that she's not interested in Timric at all, she couldn't breed one but not the other because human women don't have control of when they release pheromones like Draconian women. When we're aroused it just happens. Miss Kendra and I are going to have a little talk tonight. We need to get a handle on this before things get out of control.

I don't get a chance to speak with my sister the rest of the day, because she spends the entire day between Phan and Timric. They're getting along swimmingly and laughing it up. I'm a hundred percent sure she has no idea everyone thinks she's chosen them. I spend the day worrying about the hundred and one things on my plate, only to discover another shock when I grab a quick shower and head to bed.

Gaping at the three of them all piled into one bed, I screech, "What the hell is this?"

Kendra beams at me. "They're my protectors. We're not having sex, and I promise that I'm not getting distracted."

Folding my arms across my chest, I deadpan back sarcastically. "Well, shacking up with two guys seems distracting to me."

"It's not. We're working as a unit and getting more done as a team than we could individually. It's called synergy."

"How far back in ancient Earth history did you have to go to dig up that term?"

I get the stubborn chin up gesture from Kendra. The one she gives when she's being intractable. "Don't be angry. I have a right to make choices for myself. Besides we're not mated. We're just getting to know each other a bit better."

"I'm your guardian, and I say no." Scowling at the two younger warriors, I growl, "Get lost, both of you."

"They aren't leaving. Protectors never abandon their post."

"This would be all kinds of cute if we didn't have that important thing to do." I give her a meaningful look to remind her we're supposed to be checking on our family.

"We both have the same goal. We're just going about it different ways."

"It's always been you and me against the world."

"Well, we're in space now, and it's the four of us against the 'verse."

I can see she's not going to change her mind, and I'm too exhausted to argue with her about it. I give the three of them my back and crawl into bed. I hope now soon we get an actual room. Sleeping in the loading bay is no picnic. Turning over, tears sting in my eyes. I'm slowly losing control of this situation, and I don't know how to muscle things back into line. Why did Kendra have to get all google-eyed over guys now? Also, why did she have to mark the second one? That was totally unnecessary.

I try to fall asleep, but all I can hear is the sound of whispering from the other bed. Well, whispering and giggling. They're just too young to be thinking about mating.

My eyes grow heavy, and I get sucked into a dark dream world. My dream starts out well, so I relax into it. I'm lying on my back staring up at the stars. We're on Earth. I know because I can see the big dipper. A gentle breeze blows over me, turning slightly more chilly as the stars twinkle overhead. I'm content knowing we made it back to Earth, and then I realize I haven't checked on my family.

The wind turns bitter, and seems to be clawing at my skin. Bolting upright, I look around. Spread around on the ground is my kin, all pasty white with white eyes. They are stiff and covered in spider webs. Rolling to my feet, I go from one to another, trying to find my mother and sisters. They are nowhere to be found.

I've covered some distance checking the bodies strewn about, and now I'm near the cave my family was using for a safe house. Standing slowly, I begin walking towards the mouth of the cave. I'm expecting it to be dark, like it was when I left. It's not. There is a roaring fire just inside the mouth of the cave. The closer I get, the larger the flames become. By the time I'm standing at the mouth of the cave, it's a raging inferno. I hear my mother crying out for help, but I can't get to her. When I try to push past the flames, they lick my skin, leaving behind black searing marks on my skin. It's like the flame is alive and wants to keep me away. I can hear my sisters screaming as the flames reach out and wrap around my arms. It's shaking me, taunting me, and there's nothing I can do.

Suddenly, I jolt awake to someone shaking me. It's Kendra, with a wide-eyed young male on each side of her. I jerk back out of her grasp and scramble to the far side of my bed.

She holds up both hands in a gesture I recognize as her wanting me to calm down. "You just had another bad dream. Everything's fine."

I'm gulping air, shaking, and can't quite pull myself together. I give my head one shake to the side, trying to clear my mind. A shadow moves near the door of our tent. Instead of Tabor, it's the older warrior, Scarn. He moves to my side, wrapping a blanket around my shoulders. "Come back to bed, my queen. I will watch over you."

His voice is deep and fatherly. He's right, of course. I'm freaking out the young adults when I should be setting a positive example. Some role model I'm turning out to be. I murmur, "Thanks Elder Scarn. It's kind of you to intervene."

"Think nothing of it. You need your sleep. We have a mission to complete."

"You're right." I climb back onto my bed, even as Kendra, Phan and Timric head back to bed. I notice she's sleeping at the head of the bed under the blankets, and her companions are sleeping at the foot above the blankets. Kendra's no fool. I should have known she would take it slow.

 iftOff

~ Tabor ~

We've repaired the ship and Queen Kearney has rendered final payment to the Denarians. Phan and Timric have both snagged small six-person shuttles and the parts they need to repair them. I suspect they intend to use them as special projects to while away our time in space. It will give them something productive to do and keep them from making mischief or irritating the older warriors, so to my mind it is a good idea.

Queen Kendra seems to be welded in place between the two of them. I never see one without the other two. Phan seems happier than I can ever remember him being. Perhaps I have misjudged the situation, and she intends to breed them both. Old suspicions die hard for a battle-hardened warrior like myself. I have noticed Scarn paying more attention to our queen than ever before. He scowls at me, but does not speak his mind. I know not what to make of it.

We ready the ship for lift off. I sit in the captain's chair with Queen Kearney at my side. Today she is wearing a proper gown in honor of our first liftoff. She looks lovely, even though we brought no caretakers to see to her needs. Her hair is piled high on her head and decorated with gemstones. Even Queen Kendra is dressed like a true queen as she sits on my other side with her young males standing behind her. It's unfortunate that she elected to keep the mangy animal she played with at the salvage yard. Even now he sits at her feet, growling at anyone who looks at her.

I clear my voice and tighten my wings. "Drag, plot a course for Earth and engage on our queen's mark."

"Course laid in, sir."

Queen Kearney's voice sounds off. "Liftoff, Drag."

"Yes, my queen."

We feel barely a shudder as the gigantic ship rises from the ground. I'm pleased, because this is evidence of our mechanical skills.

Drag speaks. "Permission to break orbit."

"Granted." My queen takes to command well, clearly as proud as I am of the ship. I must admit that it pleases me to see her so happy. This is the most stress free that I can remember ever seeing her. Phan's hand comes down to land on Queen Kendra's shoulder. I'm surprised when Timric does not touch her other shoulder. Now that I think about it, she does seem to favor my brother in smiles, and she stands closer to him physically. Either my brother is her favorite, or she is still deciding and Timric has not impressed her as worthy of being mated. I don't like to think that she's toying with my brother's affections before settling down with the breeder. Now that I'm thinking more clearly, I think Queen Kendra is too nice to behave in such a way. In any event, I should not waste my time thinking about my brother's personal life but I do wish him happiness.

Scarn sounds off from the security console. "I'm picking up hyper-space signals from an incoming Strovian vessel. They are headed to Earth as well and wish to know if we would like to share their hyper-space bubble."

Queen Kearney askes excitedly. "They're one of the species that can fold space-time, right?"

I dip my head slightly in acknowledgement. "Yes, they could get us to Earth in microns instead of days but the costs will be steep."

"Don't you think it is a little convenient that they came along just when we were leaving?"

I frown. "No. This is the most prominent salvage yard within a thousand parsecs. It attracts all kind of ships. Strovians usually look for a way to offset the costs of stopping for spare parts, so it makes sense they were scanning for potential ships to share their hyper-space bubble. Even now they are likely sending out a signal offering the same to other ships."

Scarn chimes in, "They have had a Taladar vessel, a Yuroba mid-range bulk transport and a Zelerian ship accept so far. If we wish to accept their kind offer, it will cost us twenty thousand credits, and we must wait thirty microns for all the ships to converge on this location and for the Strovian ship to load the cargo being transported from the planet."

Swallowing thickly, our queen nods her head slightly. "Tell them we accept and are ready to join their hyper-space bubble when they say."

I suspect that will just about wipe out her credit account. "Would you like me to ask if they will accept some gemstone in trade?"

"Do you think they would be interested in such a trade?"

"Strovians are likely to be going to Earth for human brides. They will be interested in pleasing them with pretty baubles."

A look of relief crosses her face. "Yes, please, we have some extremely rare gemstone that should be more than enough to cover their asking price."

I type out a modest offer on my data pad and they shoot back a counter offer. I run some calculations, and we kick back and forth various deals, until I wrangle the best deal possible for my queen. We're getting the transport for a handful of her most precious gemstone and an introduction to the Earth ambassador. Little do they know, any species may request an audience with the ambassador. Sly, I know, but I am honor bound to get the best deal possible for my queen.

She's pleased when I show her my negotiation. I dash off a request for an audience with Earth ambassador, explaining that we have items to trade and are looking for luxury cloth, seeds and items for our queens in exchange for nutrient dense bars, gemstone and rare metals. I am unclear on which of our trade items gets the almost instant reply, but we set the meeting for tomorrow morning. The Strovians are more than pleased, as am I at the opportunity to show my worth as a warrior. I wish my queen to see me as a valued warrior. No sooner do I think this than she speaks.

"While we're waiting, I need to speak to you in private." I follow her to the adjoining meeting room. Kendra and her males follow us, as Scarn slips into the captain's seat. The hairs stand up on the back of my neck and I glance at my brother. He feels something is off as well. An idea gut punches me so strongly that my steps falter. Has this all been a ruse for the queens to get back to their dying world because they have no wish to live among us? I pray that is not the case.

The moment the door closes behind us, Queen Kearney turns to speak. "I spoke the truth when I said we came to Earth to trade, but trade is not our primary reason for making this journey."

I sink further down into my seat, my horns slip back against my head and my wings droop. Though I do not want to hear more, I must listen carefully. It sounds like she is leaving us.

Leaning back against the door, she explains, "Kendra and I signed the bride's registry almost two years ago in order to get money to help our family."

I jolt up in my seat and pain lances through my chest. "You have family on Earth?" Earth is a dying world, barely capable of supporting life.

She looks small and frail in the gown. It flows over her slight curves with very little effort. Her ice-blue eyes are filled with pain. She folds her arms over her chest and takes a deep breath. "We do. In fact we have a rather large family, and they are not housed in any of the bio domes or underground cities. Since we had no money, they would have been forced into the lower levels. The people there live in squalor."

"Tell me you found proper housing for them, my queen."

"We didn't. Our family owned a huge piece of property. It was almost a hundred acres covering an entire mountain. When our environment began to deteriorate, it was the oceans that soured first, turning into gigantic cesspools of acidic salt water. Then the animals began to die. Our men caught some exotic disease which locked onto their male DNA and wiped out about eighty percent of the men. There is an inoculation, but no cure. Whatever it is, the disease does not seem to affect alien visitors, so you don't have to worry about being sick."

I ask hopefully, "Are you saying that your family is still at your mountain homestead?"

She nods her head sadly. "We discovered a huge cave. It's dry and high in the mountains, which are still relatively untouched. We used to camp there on summer vacation because it had a water source."

I feel my insides crumple. "This is why you and your sister queen have pushed so hard to mine gemstone and purchase this ship. You worry about your loved ones left behind on Earth."

I watch my queen drop down into a seat. She seems relieved to get this off her chest.

"This is why you never spare time for courting warriors. You are worried about the wellbeing of your family."

"I worry that the food we left was not enough to sustain them."

Running by hands over my head, I feel my horns are now plastered to my head. My wing base aches from the tightness of my clenched wings. "This is why you and your sister queen wear uniforms instead of gowns, why you work night and day and eat only food bars."

Tears fill her eyes but she forces them back. "It's hard to wallow in luxury when your family is starving. We have little ones. The twins were newborn when we left."

I pull myself together. "We must visit them when we first arrive and see to their needs."

Phan talks for the first time. "We'll bring them to the ship so I can see to their medical needs."

Kendra reaches over and takes his hand in hers. He slips a wing around her and tugs her close.

Timric heaves in a deep breath. "My shuttle is ready. I will retrieve my bride and as many as I can carry."

My head jerks around to stare at him. However, it is Kendra who speaks. "I have a twin. She teased me that if my mate had a brother to bundle him up and save him for her."

"You have a twin?" I can scarcely imagine it.

"She looks just like me. She likes men with blond hair and Timric has a lot of it."

Suddenly everything makes sense. She chose my brother for her mate and Timric to be her sister's mate. I cannot imagine a young female who would turn down an actual breeder. "I hope she likes you as much as Queen Kendra does, Timric."

"My queen has a name. It is Kara."

"It's a good name." Turning to my queen, I murmur, "This mission is turning out to be more important than I ever imagined it would be. How many family members do you have on Earth."

She glances away. "Too many."

"Will you not trust me with a number, my queen?"

"We left behind twenty-three, all female but three. They span in age from newly born to around forty-five."

"With your approval, I will begin preparations to rescue them immediately. Can you take the bridge?"

She nods, seeming to emotional to speak. I turn to the young warriors. "Come and assist me with preparations. Leave the queens in charge of the bridge."

Timric shot out of his seat like a bolt of lightning. Phan followed him, stopping to rub his face along that of his queen. Though I don't feel we have time for sappy kissing, I wait patiently. I do this because queens require affection, and now that my brother is chosen, he is required to ensure his queen feels valued. I'm certain he wishes he could just stroll away to work with us, but he is doing is duty, and that is more important.

arth

~ Kearney ~

It seems that all our plotting, planning, and scheming has come to fruition. Our ship is in Earth's orbit, and we're loading two shuttles for descent to the surface. Since I'm human, we don't have to check in with Earth Gov first.

What seemed like such a coincidence with the Strovian vessel offering us space in their bubble when they folded space-time has turned out to be rather routine. We monitored them contacting countless other ships in orbit around Earth with similar offers when they jump back to their planet. We even discovered that for a premium price they will fall out of hyper-space at particular stops along the way, in essence allowing ships to get off at other planets. They're on a monthly run from Earth to their home planet, so if we stay a full month we can utilize their service to get most of the way back to our home world. It will cut months off our journey.

Anyways, I've tried to make contact with my family using the communication device they have but I'm not getting a reply. It could be the equipment failed, they couldn't keep it charged, or something more nefarious. I pray nothing bad happened to them. My father didn't make it to the mountain. He fell ill a while we were living in one of the bio domes. Even though we did everything we could to save him, he didn't make it. My mother was still pregnant with the twins, and that's when we decided to move to the mountains. The area of the bio dome reserved for indigent folks was filthy. There was no way my mother could have given birth there.

Living in a cave sounds awful, but it was lots cleaner than the bio dome. God, we scrubbed on that cave for days. We cleaned everything thoroughly before bringing it into the living space. I roll over everything we did to make the space habitable and feel certain we did the best we could. My big worries are that the water purification system failed or the cold weather wore them down.

I'm deep in thought until Tabor alerts me that the shuttle is packed. I'm back in a uniform for this venture. Dropping down across from Kendra, I realize how bonded she has become to Phan. They're actually pretty cute together. Timric is tense and gazing out the window. Somehow, I don't think this whole idea of picking out a guy for Kara is going to go down like Kendra thinks. She was sixteen when we left and I'm fairly certain Kara was just uncomfortable and making a joke about her sister bringing her back a mate.

Tabor is staring at me again. This time I have nothing to hide, so I smile back. His eyes get big for a second, and then he looks away. I'm getting real tired of us thinking we can tell what the other person is thinking by facial expressions and body language. I've decided to that once my family is safe, I'm going to try to get to know him better. Maybe he won't want anything to do with me but I'm going to try.

Suddenly, he bolts from his seat and grabs the control stick. We all grab onto our safety harnesses when the ship careens left. Kendra's creature roars his disapproval and jumps in front of her.

His tail whips around angrily until she reaches out a shaking hand and smooths the top of his head. "Down, Roxie." I realize for the first time that the animal is a female. Somehow she doesn't look female with the razor-sharp teeth and scruffy appearance.

I'm blasted back from my straying thoughts by another round of weapons fire, and just like that, our shuttle is blown from the sky. That shuttle had four of our fellow crew members inside, including Scarn.

"We're being fired upon from the ground." Tabor's voice is calm and controlled.

I can't keep the agitation from my voice. "Who the hell would do that?"

Darg speaks from the navigational console. "It appears to be a group of mostly males. One has a huge weapon on his shoulder. Our other shuttle didn't explode. It crashed."

I unhook my safety harness and claw my way to the console. "We need to find them before whoever in the hell fired at us finds them."

"Agreed. We were nearing the targeted landing site when the shots were fired."

"The foothills of the mountain belong to our family, and I can virtually guarantee none of them would be firing at our shuttle."

Kendra's angry voice sounds off from her seat. "Why don't we work on this little idea I've been working on called shooting back?"

I know what Commander Tabor is going to say before he opens his mouth. The group of mostly males also has women. Draconians won't fire on queens, no matter the situation.

"I advise restraint, my young queen. We know nothing of the situation below except that we are being fired upon. We have no understanding of why the queens below are directing their warriors to fire upon our shuttle. We may be violating their airspace, perhaps they fear our advanced technology or they fear our motivation for coming is not pure."

Unsnapping her safety harness, Kendra bolts forward. "Good

Lord, Kearney. Explain to him that women don't run things on Earth."

Tabor's head whips around and he asks a question that might be hysterically funny under different circumstances. "If the queens do not rule, how do the warriors get anything done?"

Darg deftly dodges another volley of shots from the ground, by gliding off to the left. That's when I see they are using laser rifles. Though I don't know how they got ahold of alien tech, I'm relieved that they ran out of rocket launchers. Thank God for small favors. I mumble to my sister, "Shielding was one of the things we apparently didn't focus much effort on since we thought Earth was a safe zone."

"It looks like things have changed over the last two years. Can you scan for our crew?"

Tabor is already doing that, and seeing his bulky frame leaning over the view screen is making it impossible for anyone else to see what's going on. "I am reading heat signatures on three survivors. We must have lost a warrior in the crash. The remaining warriors appear to be unloading their cargo onto hover boards. They will likely take flight and head for the cave with the provisions."

"Let's do another pass over my hostile counterparts. Stay out of range of their weapons this time. I want to zoom in and see if I recognize any of them."

"It will be as you say, my queen."

I sigh, cause I'm getting real tired of hearing that particular response. I need to think of a good title for myself. When we come back around, we still can't get a good look, so Tabor drops a small drone. It gets close enough to capture footage before it gets shot down. When he brings the images up on his screen, I know what the problem is.

Kendra's angry voice explains before I can manage it. "It's the Grayson clan, still as welcoming as ever. They own the property that butts up against ours and we've had nothing but a lifetime of problems from them. They fight about everything but nothing more viciously than property rights."

"Since he owns the valley below our mountain it makes sense that he's standing on our property shooting at us. His land is practically uninhabitable now."

Kendra huffs out an exasperated breath. "Not that ours is much better, but I get your point. The question is, what are we going to do about it?"

"They don't know it's us. They might be inclined to have a conversation if we can figure out a way to communicate."

Phan walks the back of shuttle and opens a crate. When he pulls out a carton of food bars, my wheels start turning. I've seen the Draconian equivalent of chalk in what I think of as their junk drawer. They use it to mark areas of the ship that need repairs. I grab it and mark on the outside of the box.

Since when does the Grayson clan shoot at their neighbors? Signal if you want to talk.

I sign it with my first and last name, and we attach a drone to the top. All cartons containing shelf stable edible items have a graphic of the particular food item in bold face on the bottom. It's done specifically so that people will recognize it as food when it's dropped from above.

We drop the carton, wait ten minutes and release another drone. I see one of them waving a dingy white shirt. "Take us down."

Tabor's mouth presses into a firm line, but he executes my order without comment. We careen into a slow downward spiral, landing on the relatively flat land leading up our mountain. It's technically our property but the Grayson clan are crawling all over it. When the shuttle doors open, we exit with me and Kendra in the lead, our warriors at our back and her newly acquired animal jumping for joy at being out of the shuttle. I'm worried that we're going to make a pretty unusual presentation until I see our neighbors. They're filthy, their clothing is rags, and they look exhausted.

I recognize old man Grayson and shout out to him. "Howdy, neighbor. Hope your wife is well, Virgil."

He steps forward, even though one of the women claws at his arms to stay back. We can't possibly look that dangerous. "Is that you, Keary girl?"

He's always shortened my name, only now I don't mind so much. "It's me, and you've got nothing to fear from us. We've brought medical supplies and fresh water, in addition to food bars."

"I'll be damned. Your ma's been saying for two damn years that you'd be back, and here you are. I see you got a whole parcel of aliens with some mighty big weapons. Why don't you tell them to leave their guns in the shuttle?"

"How's about I don't. Did you just shoot one of my shuttles out of the air, or did I imagine it?"

The old man pulls on his long grey beard. "Now I reckon we did. There ain't no debating that fact."

"You killed one of our crew."

"Now, we didn't know it was you come home to roost. The aliens that visit our world make trips out to isolated places like our mountain to rescue women. They claim they've been left out in the cold. The thing is, they don't always ask if she wants rescued. Sometimes they just take them. We've got a right to protect our womenfolk."

"I understand that, but I don't want any more trouble out of your clan while I'm here. We'll leave some supplies for you, but I want you off our land for now."

"Well the thing is, this ain't your land anymore, Keary. Your ma got hard up and traded it to us."

I'm growing ever more suspicious of his accounting of the facts. "Traded it for what exactly?"

"Protection."

Suddenly, I'm livid. He's probably been bleeding them dry all this time. My family of women and boys would have hard time standing up to him and his sons. "Where's my family, old man?"

Jerking his chin up, he responds casually. "There're still up there in their cave. Everything else belongs to us, from the ground to the sky, though." He stops, hesitating and licks his lips. "If you want to keep traveling over our land and through our sky, you'll have to pay a toll."

I'm starting to hate on this man, or rather picking up on my hating on him from before I left. It's hard to remember exactly why I ever felt guilty about hating on him. He's always been kind of a bastard, but times are tough. I get that, I really do. If there's one thing I know, it's that poverty can make people small, selfish and mean. Still, I refuse to implode what little good will is flowing between us until I speak with my mother.

"What exactly is your price, Virgil?"

"Ten cases of food bars, a medical kit with antibiotics and a water purifier to start with. Then we negotiate something new every single day you stay on our land." He stops talking, probably because I'm having a hard time keeping the anger off my face. "Don't go lookin' at me like that, Keary girl. You know I got a lot of folks in my clan that needs food and water to survive."

"You've always taken more than your share, Virgil. We both know that."

He flings his arms wide. "Look around girlie, ain't none of us lasting long on this world. Another generation or two and there ain't gonna be nothing left of my clan."

Damn it all to hell. He's right. "I'll pay your toll, Virgil. Come on over and let our medic check you out and we'll gather up your supplies."

"You wouldn't be trickin' me, would you, girl?"

"Hell no. It ain't for lack of wanting to. It's because you're right. Our life's gone to hell. There ain't no reason for us to be at each other's throats. I gotta warn you that if I find out you're directly responsible for hurting my family, that will change."

"I ain't done nothin' to warrant retaliation. You can ask her yourself."

"Come on over then. I want to get this transaction over with so I can check on our family."

They move forward cautiously, but my crew is ready. Several warriors creep out slowly, wrapping blankets around their women. Tabor unloads the exact things he asked for, only we don't have a water purification unit.

I sit on the damp ground while Phan examines Virgil. "We don't have a water purification unit with us. We leave you ten gallons of drinking water and see about getting you a filter down here tomorrow."

"That would be mighty fine, Keary. Just don't get with your family and forget about us. We got newborns to think about and we need that filter."

"I promise, we won't forget. Do you know how my family's doing?"

"That ma of yours is stubborn as ever. We tried to get them to come down and join our clan, but they refused. She kept saying you were coming back with help." Eyeing Phan and his equipment, he added. "I guess she knew what she was talking about all along."

Kendra's animal trots over and sits scratching his neck with one meaty paw.

"What the hell do you call that?"

"She's just some animal that Kendra took a liking to on an alien planet we visited. I suppose she's the alien version of a junkyard dog. The planet was a gigantic salvage yard."

"You know I used to own a salvage yard, don't ya?"

Offering him a hydration pouch from a box Timric is passing around, I nod. "Sure, I remember. People used to come from miles around to look for parts. Folks say you drove a pretty hard bargain back in the day."

The old man smiles and reaches out to pet Roxie on the head. He doesn't sip his drink, he sucks it down. I offer him the one I haven't even opened because his eyes are hollowed out and he honestly looks dehydrated. When he accepts it with a gruff thanks, a thought pops into my mind.

"Have you ever thought of leaving Earth?"

He eyes me suspiciously. "Where in the hell would we go? The only ships offering free transport off this rock and sanctuary on their planets are ones looking for women. I ain't about to give my kin up to aliens who want to make them baby factories."

"Well, you know it's not like that. There has been so few men, women are dying to find alien husbands."

"I ain't got nothing against alien men. I know there are good ones and bad ones, just like with humans. The thing is, when our womenfolk are millions of miles away on some alien planet we ain't got no way to tell if they're being mistreated, now do we?"

"I suppose not. What if you could have your own ship and go wherever you wanted?"

"Forget that, Keary girl. If you got your shuttles at an alien junk yard, you got scammed. We blasted right through one of them. I don't know how you fly them in space."

"Shuttles are like cars that fly. We use them to get from our ship to Earth and back again. Our ship has shields. We were still working on the shuttles and didn't think we needed shields on Earth."

"Who owns the ship you got up there, girl? You or your alien friends."

"Kendra and I own the ship. These men are our crew members."

He squeezes the last bit out of his hydration pack and sucks it down before responding. "Shit, I don't know nothing about spaceships."

"We didn't either. We learned. Your sons and daughters can learn just like we did. You hire people to run the ship, just like a corporation hires employees to work for them."

"If I find myself a gold mine, I'll be sure to think about buying a ship."

Glancing around at all his kin, I lean over and whisper. "You've got something better than gold."

He shakes his head, "I already told you I'm not trading my kin."

I run my hands through my hair a couple of times. "The aliens who run the junkyard, trade in more than just junk. I got a third off my ship because we donated hair."

Phan chimes in, "Some species use it in their cloning technology. They don't make exact replicas of people. They use it to grow more diverse clones and for organ regeneration."

We continue to talk about space and our new home world with Virgil. The old man can't seem to keep his hands off Roxie. It makes me sad that the only animals left on Earth are protected species in zoos. Having a pet is a small luxury the old man probably enjoyed at one time.

nee Deep In Queens

~ Tabor ~

As we usher the queens back onto the ship, I am in awe of my queen. She possesses the diplomatic skills of an ambassador. I watched her turn a mortal enemy into an ally in a few microns. The older man started off gruff and disrespectful, but Queen Kearney had him practically eating out of her hand by the time our transaction was completed.

I'm strangely intrigued by her idea for the clad of Grayson to trade biological matter for a small ship. A large family could just about make a fine living with such a ship. Why should they be forced to suffer and die on a barren planet if it can be prevented?

At first, I did not understand Queen Kearney's plan, but now it all makes sense. I hope she plans to take her family from this dying world. The oceans churn with acid and pollution, there are no animals running free and wild, and our scans reveal that on some parts of the planet one cannot breathe without a respirator to protect from the particulate matter floating in the air. This is no place to birth young.

Seeing the hopeless expressions on the Grayson clade's faces affected me deeply. I will render whatever assistance is necessary to see them safe. From the tight expressions on the other warriors, I suspect they feel the same as me. Seeing their frail females would have been enough to engage our services.

It takes only moments for us to reach the cave site by shuttle. We find our three warriors there caring for the females. They have built a fire using heating gel and the females are all huddled in warm blankets. Each has a hydration packet in her hands and a food bar in her lap. I realize some of the youngsters are male, the oldest just breaking into adolescence.

A woman screeches and several jump from their seats to run to the sister queens. One is a mature queen who was sitting with Elder Scarn. He is left grappling with two youngsters who can't be more than a couple of seasons old. Suddenly, everyone is on their feet, moving into a tight circle around the sister queens. I have rarely seen so many queens in one place and looking so rough.

One of the three crew members who arrived first directs my attention to a floating hover board. It has the body of the crew member we thought was dead. He has a stasis strip running down his body. I can see it sticking out the top of the blanket. Why they have wasted a blanket on a person in stasis is beyond my ability to reason. "Warm blankets should have gone to the queens."

Ledan glances over his shoulder at the tangle of queens. "The elder queen insisted. I do not believe she understands how stasis fields work, Commander Tabor."

I know he's probably referring to the sister queen's mother, but she is not of age to be considered an elder. "Remove the supplies from our shuttle and take a team back to repair our downed shuttle. Our queen has made peace with the hostile natives and they are to be treated with respect."

Never one to second-guess the judgement of a queen, Ledan dips his head in submission and jogs off to assist the crew members who are already unloading supplies. I begin exploring the area, looking for danger and security threats. Their cave is spacious and there is a large flat area that juts out the front. This is where the queens were warming themselves. I'm confused about why the warriors built their fire outside the cave. The heat source they are using could easily heat the interior of the cave. I guess the queens did not wish to be indoors.

Scarn approaches me with a child under each arm. He smiles and they are laughing. "What have you there, my friend?"

"A young warrior and a young queen who thinks she is a warrior. Where shall I put them, commander?"

"I would have to say to put them down. Young warriors and queens like to run around and play."

He laughs merrily. "These two like to fly."

"If their queen mother allows it, take them under your wing and let them enjoy the fresh air."

Sighing contentedly, the scarred elder warrior states, "This will be their third trip. We should see about getting wings grafted onto their bare little backs."

Before I can answer, I am called by my queen. My feet are moving before I will them to and I am at her side in the blink of an eye.

"I wanted to introduce you to my mother. Her name is Ella."

Turning to her mother, she gestures towards me. "Mother, this is Commander Tabor. He's been looking out for us since we've been gone."

The mature queen's hair has barely a thread of gray to be seen, yet her face is wrinkled around the eyes and mouth.

She smiles at me, and her voice is kindly when she speaks. "It's nice to meet you, Commander Tabor. Thank you for looking out for my girls."

I drop to my knee in submission and bow my head.

"Oh goodness, not you too."

My queen explains quietly. "I told you, it's just their way of communicating that they'll submit to your wishes."

"That's real nice, but he needs to get up and talk to me like a gentleman. I've got a bunch of questions."

I rise to my feet and greet her verbally like she prefers. "Forgive our gestures of submission. I have no wish to make you uncomfortable."

"It's no problem, but from now on, I want you on your feet talking to me. Humans prefer respectful conversation over displays of submission."

"This I will remember, queen mother. You mentioned that you wished to ask me questions. What would you like to know?"

"My daughter says you are all dragon warriors. Does that mean you turn into dragons?"

My queen shifts from one foot to another, looking uncomfortable.

I answer honestly because not only do I have no reason to do otherwise, but lying to a queen mother is a crime punishable by death among my people. "In ancient times, our people had their genome spliced with that of dragons. Though we had fire in our blood and could start a fire with our breath, it was determined that more modifications were needed. There was more splicing with an unknown species. The result is we no longer have fire in our blood but each family line is gifted in one way or another."

Glancing curiously between me and her daughter, she asks, "What is your family's gift?"

Pressing my hand to my chest, I answer as best I can. "We sense danger in the heat of battle. It is how I knew to move our shuttle out of the line of fire today."

"I heard all about how old man Grayson shot down one of your shuttles. I mean to have words with the old coot about that."

"I believe Queen Kearney has already done that."

"Queen Kearney?"

My queen jumps into the conversation and explains. "They call all women queens, mother, not just me."

She takes a deep breath. "You called me queen mother because I am Kearney's mother, right?"

Dipping my head again, I elaborate. "When our linguistics program broke down your language, there was no word that our elders felt communicated the esteem and respect we bear for human females. The closest match was queen. We treat females much like queens are treated on this planet."

"Their society is matriarchal."

Nodding, her expression turns somber. "I see. Kearney tells me that we would all be welcomed on your home world, and she has a ship in orbit to take us there. Is this true?"

"I do not understand the question?"

"She is double-checking to make sure my family is welcome among your people."

"Ah, I understand now. Queens command and warriors obey. It is the natural order of things."

"I don't understand any more now than I did a moment ago."

Her tone is frustrated and I cannot determine why. I try to clarify our position. "Your daughter has determined that you are welcome among us. Queens are gifted with the right of choosing, not males. No male will go against the word of a queen."

By this time Kendra, Phan and Timric are standing close. Phan supplies helpfully, "Warriors serve and protect queens. If more queens come to our world more warriors will have something to do."

"How about the boys? Are they welcome as well?"

"I do not know how helpful a warrior can be without wings, but our numbers are few so any assistance they could provide in serving and protecting queens would be greatly appreciated."

"It's my understanding there are more women than men. Aren't you afraid they'll take mates away from your kind if we relocate?"

I step back into the conversation. "Males may not take queens. They must wait to be chosen. Whether a queen chooses a human mate or a Draconian mate, it makes no difference because the decision is hers. I am inclined to say most warriors would wish the queens to have more selection because it is not right to deny a queen."

Kearney's irritated voice chimes in. "Except the two women who rule our new home world have specifically asked for women to relocate. Male children are very welcome. Adult males, not so much. Until we get a chance to talk to them about that, we'd best stick to just our family."

"I see. So the Grayson's are shit out of luck when it comes to getting rescued?"

At this point Kearney just seems tired. "I have an idea for getting them off Earth but I can't save everyone."

Before I can think to stop myself, my wing comes out to slip behind my queen and I pull her close. "This day has been fraught with danger and my queen has exhausted herself negotiating peace with the clade of gray beings."

Kendra murmurs, "He means the Grayson clan. Clade is Draconian for clan."

"Yes, this is what I meant. Perhaps you could speak with Queen Kendra and allow my queen to rest."

"Why is she your queen in particular?"

My queen snuggles under my wing before responding. "They all call me that because I'm in charge of the ship."

The queen mother's expression shifts into one of amusement. "Fine, take your queen and let her rest. I have many questions for my younger daughter as well."

I catch Kendra's expression and it is one I cannot identify. The brave young queen stands her ground before her mother with her warriors at her back.

I settle my queen down and make her a warm drink from one of the crates I packed. She is with her family, so now she can eat and drink like a normal person. Our drink is similar to the drink humans call simulated coffee, except it's warm and nourishing. I make a large vat of it and begin passing out drinks in collapsible cups. I keep a watch over my queen as I make food for her and her family to eat.

My brother stands by his queen, answering all the queen mother's questions as best he can. Whatever he tells her must have pleased her, because she reaches out to embrace him and then her young daughter. When I hand my queen her food, she thanks me. "We're really happy to have a doctor in the family. Don't worry, you'll end up with a hug before it's all said and done as well."

That clarifies the situation for me. I had the thought the hug was a welcome to her family gesture, rather than simply showing approval for his vocational choice. Though Phan is beaming, Timric appears confused. It occurs to me search the faces for the one who shares Kendra's face. Her twin is not to be found among the queens. Stooping down in front of Queen Kearney, I ask, "Where is your sister queen, Kara. She is not here."

She grabs my shoulder. "Don't freak out." Her voice is loud and stern, drawing notice from the others.

"Tell me now, my queen."

"Calm down. She went to town to trade some pine nuts for medication for one of the little ones."

I'm stunned. "You have a sick child in this group?"

"Phan already scanned and healed her. What part of calm down don't you understand, big guy?"

"Your sister queen is in the city, unprotected."

"She'll be fine in the bio dome."

"She should not be unprotected. Queens are few and precious."

Giving my arm a jerk, she frowns. "Not around here. On Earth women are man and males are few. I know that's not how it works in the rest of the world, but it's true for this planet."

Timric is at my side in a flash. "You are correct, Commander. I wish to find my queen and shelter her under my wing."

I stand and begin brainstorming ways to find the missing queen. "We will get Phan to load Kendra's biological signature into hand held scanners and..."

Queen Kearney comes to her feet as well. "You guys are not going to let this go, are you?"

Our heads swivel around to face her at the same time. My brain is scrambling for something to say to get her to recognize how serious of a problem having a young sister queen unprotected in a large city can be. In many ways my queen is innocent. I have traveled the verse and know very well how danger can creep up on a queen before she realizes. Another thought pops into my head. "Is she the only family member missing from your ranks?"

The queen mother wanders over, clearly having overheard our conversation. "I have a niece who works in one of the restaurants in town as a cook. She doesn't get off until midnight."

I try not to be abrasive to the queen mother, but I'm unable to hold my tongue. "My language translator is telling me midnight is a time point which occurs during the dark of night. May I suggest that we retrieve your daughter immediately and if the niece queen is not agreeable to leaving her workplace, we will leave warriors and a shuttle to escort her back to this grouping?"

"I think all that's a bit of an overkill, but if you need security to be tight, I'm agreeable to your suggestion."

Turning my attention to Queen Kearney, I bow my head respectfully. "Do I have your leave to see to the safety of the two errant queens as well, my queen?"

"Well, they're not really errant, but sure, what the heck. Knock yourself out. Just don't scare the hell out of them. Huge warriors dropping out of nowhere might freak them out a little."

Timric interjects earnestly, "We have no wish to distress the queens. We will be careful to ensure they are not frightened and respect their wishes."

Phan is already loading a hand held scanner so we can match to her biological signature. Of course, we have eyes and can recognize her by sight since she is Kendra's twin, but with our hand held, we can scan large areas. I turn to Queen Kearney. "I will leave Elder Scarn and the remaining warriors to protect you. Ledan should be returning with your second shuttle once the repairs are made."

"I'm going to focus our time on packing. I want us up out of here as soon as possible. We might be able to fit everyone into the two shuttles. If not, I'll leave the warriors and come back for them."

"That is a wise decision, my queen." For some reason I do not know, I reach out and draw her to me. "All will be as you say. We will have your family safe aboard your vessel before the sun rises on another day."

"That's just what I wanted to hear." She's gazing at me in a way that makes my cock ache. I am a dishonorable warrior for thinking of my queen this way, when all she wants is my protection.

Her hands come up to rest on my hips, and she moves closer. "Now that my family is safe, everything changes."

"I will obey. This is my vow to you."

A smile lights up her face. "You say the most adorable things. Don't go looking at other ladies when you're in the bio dome. I won't have it."

Her statement feels possessive. "I wish only to secure your loved ones and rush back here to look at you."

My mouth is saying things that make little sense and that my brain does not fully approve of, but I care not as long as my queen's attention is focused squarely upon me.

"Get going, you big Romeo. I want you to rush, but be safe doing it."

"I will return quickly. Do you wish me to secure any extra provisions while we are in the trading center?"

"We call it a marketplace, and buy whatever you think best. After we link the Strovians with the ambassador, I plan to do some large-scale trading."

"As you wish, my queen." Instinct tells me to brush my face against her cheek so she will feel my affection, but I doubt my queen thinks of me like that. Therefore, I step back and turn to Timric. "Are you ready?"

"More than ready, Commander."

etting Reacquainted

~ Kearney ~

We watch the shuttle take off with Tabor and Timric. My mother ushers everyone back down and we sit and sip our hot drinks. Phan seems worried and Kendra picks up on it immediately. "Hey, don't worry about your brother. He's going to be fine. Earth Gov has a zero-tolerance policy for harming aliens. They don't want anything interfering with the trade they bring."

"I should have gone with him to find your kin, but I did not wish to leave you unprotected."

Scarn's gruff voice sounds off. "You're newly mated. The mate bond is strong and instinctual with our kind. I do not believe you could have forced yourself from her side even if you were ordered to do so."

Phan's wings flutter in a clear gesture of frustration. "We are not yet mated." I can tell admitting to that fact pained his soul.

Scarn frowns, as he wrestles with Roxie with one hand. "I do not smell a mating scent, yet you have been on your queen's sleeping platform every night."

Before our mother can ask, I do. "I remember hearing something about how the warriors release a certain scent to lure their mates, but to be honest, I never quite understood it."

"During the courting phase, when there is intimacy between a warrior and a queen, she releases pheromones, and it triggers the male to release his mating scent. It is automatic. Some males claim they can control the release of their mating scent, but I think they are confused. The queen mates her warrior several times in rapid succession and when his eggs release, the scent dissipates."

My mother wrinkles her nose in a delightfully pensive expression. "That's weirdly fascinating. Do you have any idea why that happens?"

Scarn sighs, clearly unaccustomed to having to talk about mating so openly.

Phan answers the question for him. "Some say our mating scent is a leftover remnant of our dragon DNA. Others, such as myself, believe it's an evolutionary advantage to ensure the survival of our line. Our mating scent is pleasing to queens but thoroughly repugnant to other warriors. It ensures other warriors do not approach a queen when she is mating. Some males are convinced their scent is what lured their mate to them in the first place, but I do not think that is the case."

I'm slowly trying to work out why he isn't releasing his scent. "So if Kendra doesn't get aroused by you, what will happen? Will you two break up so she can find a guy who excites her more?"

Kendra's annoyed voice hisses at me. "I'm all kinds of aroused, not that it's any of your business. You can be such a busybody sometimes. You know that, right?"

"I'm not trying to embarrass your new beau. This is kind of all-new information to me, and I'm just trying to understand it."

Scarn broke in again. "Phan is a young warrior. It is likely that in his ambition to lure a queen he didn't realize that his hormones haven't come in yet. Sometimes that does not happen until the warrior has seen twenty summers."

I feel terrible for Phan, because it's clear that he is humiliated by his situation.

Kendra just giggles. "Well that puts him a step ahead of all the other warriors. He's got his queen in place before he needs her." She grabs his hand and grins up at him.

He must have appreciated the humor of his own situation after all. His face brightens in an instant. "So, you are keeping me?"

"Of course. Do you see me hanging on any other hot warriors?"

His wings relaxed and his horns perked back up. "I do not."

"I'm not only keeping you, I'm making you my Takadon."

I explain for my mother. "I think that means he'll be her one and only male. Some women take more than one husband. Choosing a Takadon means he's highly esteemed and when they're joined together, they'll be inseparable."

My mother looks to Scarn, who nods like a human. "What your daughter queen says is true. Among our people it is the highest honor a queen can bestow upon a warrior."

Phan's wings flutter with excitement, and he can't keep the smile off his face. "I promise to be the best Takadon ever. You will not regret taking me to you, my queen."

Naturally, Kendra lights up like a Christmas tree. "Don't tell me what I already know, handsome."

"I never thought I would be selected for mating, much less that I would be chosen to be Takadon by such a beautiful and fun-loving queen. I am finding our mating to be more than I could have imagined in my strangest dream. Entares has smiled upon me and I am more grateful than I have words to say."

Our mother laughed as she gazed at the young healer. "You seem to find very appropriate words to describe your feelings. You both have my congratulations again."

I clear my throat and gesture towards the cave. "Why don't you two lovebirds make yourself useful and help everyone pack. I want to lift off the moment Commander Tabor gets back with Kara and Laura."

Scarn stands, dusting off his pants. "Come younglings, I will assist you and organize this endeavor." Turning to me he drops his head slightly. "All will be as you command, Queen Kearney."

"It was more a request than a command, but thanks Scarn. I appreciate all your hard work and patience answering our question about mating."

His eyes jump from me to my mother and then dart away. He begins backing away. "I am at your service, Queen Kearney."

As they wander off, I frown.

"What's bothering you, Kearney?"

"Just the thousand and one unspoken alien customs I don't really understand yet." She raises one brow and waits for me to elaborate.

"He's always called me my queen until just now." I shrug. "Suddenly I'm Queen Kearney now."

"I've noticed the only men who don't say *my queen* are the ones with mates or hope to be getting mates shortly, like Timric." My mother gives me a meaningful look and I palm smack my own forehead. "He's interested in someone."

My mother replies cheerfully. "Well someone is definitely interested in him. Only time will tell though."

I'm agog that my mother might be interested in the elder warrior. "He's old, you do know that don't you?"

"Chasseing after the twins reminds me that I'm no spring chicken either. Let's talk about what I really want to hear. "What is it really like living with aliens?"

"They're real nice. I don't like how they expect us all to wear gowns and acquiesce to their never-ending pampering. It gets old. I feel like Kendra and I were the odd girls out on their planet because we didn't do all that."

"When in Rome, do as the Romans. I think that's the expression that fits this situation. They're being kind enough to take us in, not the other way around. I don't expect us to change any of our core values, but I expect us to make a good-faith effort to integrate into their culture. It's not fair to move there and force them all to live according to our customs."

My eyes slide away, because my kind-hearted mother has hit the nail right on the head. She must sense I need a minute to process that information, because she smiles brightly and shifts the conversation to my love life. "That Commander Tabor is impressive. He seems really protective of you. Are you and the good commander sparking up a little romance?"

"I wish that were the case, because I certainly wouldn't mind getting to know him. However, after the whirlwind affair with Kendra and Phan, I don't think they date. You're either bobbing around on the edges of their notice, or you're the center of their world. There's no dating or in between that I can see."

My mom responds cautiously. "They made it pretty clear that the women do the pursuing in relationships, and just whatever they decide is fine with everyone."

I roll my eyes in exasperation. "It's even worse than that. They literally think women can do no wrong. No matter what we do, they just reorganize everything around our wishes. The only push back you get is what you just saw. It's always related to our safety and security."

"I'm gonna need more detail on that, Keary."

I think how to best explain a Draconian male's devotion to a queen. "On the new Draconian home world, they have a fancy building, kind of like a hotel, that they put the women up in. They have a swimming pool and have fancy dinners. The women all wear beautiful gowns, because the males believe they need to be outfitted in clothing equal to their beauty."

"That sounds like a bit much."

"They're very particular about how women are treated. Kendra and I refused gowns and spent all our time mining for gemstone to purchase our ship. We worked about twenty hours, and slept rough on the ground near the mining pit for ten hours, for months. We were used to camping, and the weather was chilly only at night."

"Still, that's quite a sacrifice."

"Not really, but that's not the point I'm making. Instead of pushing us to go to the luxury housing, Tabor just brought us tons of warm bedding, kept a fire going, and helped us grade and sell our gemstone to get the most money for our hard work. When I said I wanted a ship, he didn't ask questions. He just signed right up for my crew and began helping me make that happen."

"Really? That sounds like he likes you."

"In the beginning, I think he was just on automatic pilot. He wasn't joking when he said queens command and warriors obey. Most of the men on their home world have been horribly abused by their own queens before escaping to this sector of space." I lean close and lower my voice. "I heard from one of the other women that their queens had symbionts. The symbionts were more like parasites, and were called soul suckers. They fed on pain and misery, so they dealt as much of it to the males as possible."

My mother's expression is a little perturbed. She wraps her arms around her waist and shudders. "It seems like something from a horror movie."

"They even went so far as to kill the hatchlings the warriors spawn if they are not perfect."

Mother shot me an annoyed look. "I think you've just crossed the line from believable to unbelievable."

"Think about it, mother. Timric comes from a long line of breeders. They can spawn up to ten or twelve young at a time, yet his father only has four living children from three different spawnings. They call what their queens did "a reaping." It was done several times before the young hatched, and I suspect it was designed to provoke the maximum amount of grief for the father. Imagine how painful that was for the men."

My mother rubs her temple. When she speaks, her voice is a whisper. "If the symbionts fed off pain, that would have kept them sated for a very long time. I never thought such cruelty existed in the universe."

"I think they have been exposed to the worst the 'verse has to offer. That's why they are so protective of us. We're nothing like their abusive queens, and they are drawn to make sure we never suffer like they have. I'm concerned that if we're not careful we could really take advantage of their pain and eagerness to protect us."

"That would be horrible. I'll have a talk with our family members, and make sure they know to moderate their expectations and not to keep pushing your crew for more favors."

My anxiety clicks down, and I realize that I'm fighting back tears. "These men are really good people, and I just don't want anyone letting our good fortune go to their heads."

"I can see they've done right by you and Kendra. I promise you that we'll make this work. Do you have a plan at this point?"

"Yes. We got here really quickly, because we hitched a ride with an alien ship that folded space-time. They're not coming back this way for another month. I was hoping to see if any other women want to hitch a ride, and maybe trade some of my gemstone for household stuff and seeds for my hydroponics unit."

"I know a seed bank where we could get seeds. Since planting is has become difficult, they're not in big demand anymore."

"I'm glad the twins are doing well. You can't imagine how much I worried over them these last couple of years."

"To be honest, Virgil went the extra mile to make sure we got what we needed to get by. I don't know if it was his bright idea or Donna's, but he found a job for Laura and scrounged parts for our equipment when things broke."

"He made you sign over our land though, didn't he?"

My mother heaves in a deep breath, and her eyes fill with tears. "We've been as much friends as enemies. Though I honestly hate dealing with him, he's come through for us more than once when things were really bad. If we can do anything for his clan, I'd appreciate seeing it done."

"I've already planted a seed in his mind. I'll give him a few days to see if it takes root."

"What kind of plan?"

"One where he gets a small trade ship and crew of his own. He had a hard time getting his head around the idea when I broke it all down for him."

"It seems like an absurd idea."

"It's the only one I've got at the moment." I reach out and take my mother's hands in mine. When we're standing there face-to-face, I drop the biggest bomb ever. "Being in space is really weird. Things happen that you don't see coming, and often times those things don't make any sense. We've had to kind of roll with the punches, think on our feet, and not get hung up on questioning things that don't matter in the general scheme of things."

"I get what you're saying. We need to modify out expectations and be ready for anything."

Nodding, I answer honestly. "That's it in a nutshell. One minute we think it's gonna take months to get back to Earth and the next we're bartering passage with an alien ship that folds space-time for a handful of gemstones and a formal introduction to the Earth ambassador. The thing is, I never knew ships could fold space-time, and anyone can get a meeting with the ambassador, just for asking."

"I see how that doesn't make much sense."

"I just try to stay flexible in my thinking, and make the best decision I can in real time. That's what we're all gonna have to do to survive."

"I tend to agree that the strangeness of space and alien worlds beats dying out on a world that's slowly becoming uninhabitable."

"If you want, I'll talk to Virgil myself and explain things to him."

I waggle my eyebrows. "We should start with Donna. His new wife is a good listener."

Mom bursts out laughing, and it cheers my heart to know we're finally together and on the same page.

he Bio Dome

~ Tabor ~

We touched down on the one of landing pads near the bio dome and headed in through the huge front entrance. Surprisingly, they allow us to keep our weapons, saying it is because Draconians have been inducted to the Intergalactic Council of Planets. We upload a map of the city and head for their trading center.

We see mostly queens. The general population appears to be approximately ten percent male, and few appear to be warriors. It is no wonder that the females of this world wish to find alien mates. We get curious looks, admiring looks, and some disapproving looks from the human population. It does not surprise me to find that some do not wish aliens to visit their world, for I have never met a species that agreed all on a single thing. Humans are no different in this regard.

We use the hand scanner to locate the sister queen, Kara. She is standing near a stall haggling with a vendor. We approach her cautiously; concerned that she might not wish to speak to strangers. Before I could get a world out, Timric steps forward to speak to her. "Forgive the interruption Queen Kara. You sister queens have tasked us with escorting you back to your homestead."

Rather than answer him, she turned her back on us and continues negotiating with the vender. It bothers me that she is trading her limited foodstuffs for medication she does not need. She does not know Phan already healed the child in question. We wait patiently for her to conclude her transaction because there is nothing else we can do in this situation.

I am used to warriors resembling their sires. Both Phan and I closely resemble our sire. It is a little disconcerting to see a female with another female's face. I realize in the blink of an eye that I think of queens as individuals and warriors as less than unique. It seems so wrong now that I think about it.

The beautiful queen that I am growing every day more obsessed with is almost as protective of us as we are of her. She didn't wish me to seek out her sister queen in the city because she worried for me being a stranger to her world. I remember the way she permitted my brazen touch and even put her hands upon me in return. An idea sparks in my mind.

When Queen Kara is finished with her transaction, she slips the vial of medication into a small bag hanging from her waist. Before Timric can speak, I step forward again. "Queen Kearney gave her leave for us to watch over you while you go about your business today and escort you back to her."

She eyes us suspiciously. "I'm not going anywhere with two complete strangers."

"Your mother even agreed that our presence was a good idea. Queen Ella is a lovely and gracious queen mother."

Hearing us speak her mother's name buys us a moment of her time. "Who the heck are you guys?"

"I command your sister's ship. She means to take you to our home world along with all your kin in a month's time."

"That sounds pretty fantastical to me."

I pull out my handheld. "If it pleases you, I will show you images I have captured of your sister queen over the last two years. If you would like to rest, we can have a drink at whichever establishment makes you feel most comfortable. We certainly pose no danger to you in a public place."

Spinning on her heel, she states over her shoulder, "Fine, but you're buying."

I shoot Timric a quick glance and his expression is relieved. We tuck our wings tightly against our backs and keep our horns alert for danger as we follow Queen Kara to what appears to be a local saloon. Several people greet her but appear surprised that she is here. She grabs a seat near the back, and we slide into chairs on either side of her.

"I hunger. Do they serve any food here?"

"This establishment was patterned after a vintage sports bar. They sell a limited variety of foods."

I pull a metal ring, and a flat bar recessed into the tabletop pops up. The menu is attached to it and it slides up, so I order things I don't recognize as food at random from the menu. "Order what you like, Queen Kara. It is our honor to have you as a dining partner." She pecks something I cannot see, as does Timric. I link to my credit account and pay the bill. Timric spends his time staring at the small queen who looks like his best friend's mate. However, I am fascinated with our surroundings. The humans have decorated the walls with random objects, most of which I cannot identify. There are images of sports heroes on the walls as well. I must admit to losing track of time, and then someone drops drinks at our table.

The young queen speaks up. "I think you mixed us up with another table. We only have three people, and there are seven drinks."

"That's what was on the order. Do I need to take some of them back?"

She shakes her head, "I guess not. These are big guys. I guess they drink more than the average human."

"I'll have your food out shortly. If you need anything, just use the chime."

"Thanks, I appreciate it."

"No problem. You know we aim to please here at the Sports-man's Paradise."

Both queens laugh as the human tasked with serving our food sashays away.

She sips her drink and asks quietly, "Did you say you had pictures of my sister? I'd like to see them please."

"I would be happy to show them to you. You could also talk to your sister queens."

"Are you serious? I would love that!"

I grab my hand held and pull up my queen's frequency. A holographic image of Queen Kearney comes up almost immediately. She's smiling and happy like I've never seen her. "Did you find Kara, or are you still searching for her bio-signature?"

"We have found her, my queen. She wishes to speak to you."

My queen puts her fingers between her teeth and creates a high-pitched sound as she waves her arms. "Kendra get over here, the commander found Kara."

Suddenly, both of them are crowding into the view screen, all smiles and excitement. It's good to see them talking and reconnecting, but I'm anxious to get them safely to our ship.

Our food comes, and out of habit I begin putting small bits of each kind of food on a plate for Queen Kara. With a quick flick of his wrist, Timric places his knife over mine. "This is not your queen to care for, sir."

I believe he is out of line, but have no desire to stand between a warrior and a potential queen. He quickly serves the frail human queen who has only seen fit to order a drink for herself.

She closes down the line with an entirely different attitude. Though they have not discussed that Timric has been chosen for her, they have verified that my queen wishes to relocate them to our home planet. The young queen seems thrilled with the idea and has a million questions as she dives into her food. Timric navigates most of her questions, pleased to be interacting with this new queen.

"I don't think we should wait around hours for Laura to leave a job she'll never go back to anyways."

I speak up cautiously. "You did not react well to being approached by strangers. Perhaps it would be better if you make contact with Queen Laura rather than us."

She takes a moment to process my request before sucking down the rest of her drink and nodding. "I can definitely do that, and you're right in thinking she will probably respond better to me than the two of you."

I am relieved that we will not have to approach another queen without introduction this day. "Thank you Queen Kara. We wish to gather your kin with as little disruption to their daily lives as possible."

We make our way to an elaborate restaurant some distance away. Queen Kara tells the person at the door that there is an emergency, and we are to fetch her kin queen immediately. The inter-working of a queen's mind is a complete mystery to me. I would have never considered outright lying to make contact with someone, but this new queen does so without a second thought.

When the kin queen rushes out to speak with us, the two whisper with their heads together for a few minutes. Since I have the finely honed senses of a warrior, I hear enough of their words to know Queen Kara is informing her queen that they are rescued and will be leaving for our planet very soon. Her kin seems elated and skips off to alert her leader that she must leave and will not be returning. She wishes to collect something called pay. I understand this to be her wages.

We wait for a short time and she emerges without the white covering, which designates her as a food handler on this planet. After the two queens whisper together some more, Queen Kara speaks up. "Would it be possible for us to shop? Laura wants to purchase supplies for our voyage with her earnings." Looking from one to the other of us, she adds, "We'll make it quick."

Timric answers, his voice solemn. "We would be honored to escort you on whatever activities you wish. Might I suggest that we purchase a meal for your kin? She must hunger after working so hard this day."

The hardworking young queen smiles up at him. "I'd love that, but I need to shop first."

Timric pulls a nutrient dense food bar from his waist pouch and offers it to the queen along with his drink canteen. "I know this is not food fit for a queen, but it will stave off your hunger until your shopping chore is done." Turning to the queen he hopes to make his own, his demeanor softens. "It would be my honor to purchase whatever necessities or luxuries you require for your trip, my queen."

She immediately looks uncomfortable, likely thinking he is trying to lure her into a situation where she is beholden to him. I quickly speak up. "I wish to ensure my queen's family has everything they could possibly desire for our voyage. If you will but assist me in selecting items for their comfort, you will both be rewarded with whatever you like for the trip. Does that sound fair?"

Though still a little suspicious of our motivations, they nod. I know not why, but these younger queens are beginning to wear on my patience. I wish only to hasten this chore, spirit away my queen's kin to the safety of our ship, and get back to spending time with the beautiful Kearney. She is mature like me, and having her under my wing is a pleasure like no other.

The shopping turns out to be much more involved than I anticipated, and as we shop, I worry that the two young do not know enough about my queen to guide us in shopping for her. As we devour one section of the huge indoor shopping center after another, I focus on purchasing in bulk for her large family and training my eye on items my female will like best. I wish her entire family to be comfortable aboard our ship, and for that to happen, they must be outfitted with necessities from their world.

ettling In

~ Kearney ~

Tabor and Timric somehow found Kara and our cousin Laura among the thousands of humans in the bio dome, and made it home with them in about five hours. We loaded all our possessions into the shuttle that returned after being repaired.

Tabor actually came back with a boatload of merchandise. The man shops like it's his job or something. He bought specially designed metal boxes and had them welded to the bottom of our shuttle. I can only assume it is so that when it comes time to fit my family and their belongings into the shuttles, there will be room for everything. He's real considerate about most things.

I have to admit that I'm kind of curious about what's in those boxes. I expect that I'll see him wearing new clothing or something in the near future. One can only imagine why one single man would need so much stuff. On the bright side, I guess that means he loves human stuff.

All right, I'm obsessing about the hot commander, and for all I know he's just being nice to me because I'm a woman. When he ushers us into the shuttles, we all grab seats. He had benches welded to the floor with a dozen safety harnesses while he was in the bio dome. I guess Earth has started some kind of boutique business in catering to aliens. They're broke and aliens have credits so it's a win-win, I guess.

We're ready for liftoff just after the sun sets. Watching Tabor check everyone's safety harness is kind of cute. He's so careful, especially with the younger kids. I heard he promised the boys flight suits and the girls princess gowns. We'll have to see how that shakes out, cause I don't remember there being a tailor on board our ship.

Finally he comes to stand near my seat. Thrilled, I tilt my head up to look at him and he seems happy as a clam. The handsome commander's pretty easy going most of the time so that doesn't really surprise me. The only thing that really pisses him off is women being in danger, so I'm betting he's going to be pretty thrilled to have us all on the ship under his watchful eye.

Crew members near the door activate the closing mechanism and the door slowly closes off the view of my childhood campground. I get the very strong feeling this is the last time any of us will see what was once our property. Come to find out, my family didn't have much in the way of possessions, so we were able to fit the warriors and all my family into the two shuttles.

Tabor squats down to speak to me. "I had our crew on the ship prepare quarters for your family. Kara put together a list of which of your kin would be compatible for sharing space and which required private space. It appears most of them don't wish separate quarters, as it would make them sad and lonely."

"I reach out and pat his shoulder. I know Draconian women avoid each other like the plague. We're not like that."

"This I remembered. I just seems strange to stack several queens to a room."

"When things first began to go bad, our extended relatives sent their kids to us because we were the only ones in our family with property that was remotely viable. Within a short time we were forced into the caves. I'm betting that sisters and brothers want to be kept together for the voyage. They don't know our crew like I do, so they're just hedging their bets."

I can tell he's slightly confused by my hedging of bets metaphor but he gets the general message. "Your sister queens report," he continues, "that they are intent on bunking together. Therefore, I have arranged for you to have a private chamber, one befitting your station. I hope this meets with your approval?"

"It looks like I'll be on my own for the first time in a good long while. Make it clear that you are the only warrior with unrestricted access to my chamber."

His head snaps down to look at me. If he gets the hint I'm giving, he gives no indication. Instead he bows his head, murmuring, "You honor me with your trust, my queen." I sigh, cause it's clear I couldn't catch a hot warrior with a fishing pole and the patience of a saint. Looking at the structure of his handsome jawline up close makes me want to touch his skin. It's just like human skin only thicker and with different shades of green patched together to make a subtle camouflage pattern. He's got interesting spots covering his head instead of hair, and his ears have a slight point. Draconians all have horns, but they're not like I expected horns to be like. Theirs are somewhat pliant and seem to react to their moods by slipping back against their heads when they are embarrassed, contrite, or sad. Those horns perk right up when it comes time to mate or when they're angry. All-in-all, he's perfect.

Mulling over the conversation I had with my mother earlier, I decide to take her advice about respecting Draconian customs. I'll try to fix myself up and wear more gowns for a couple of reasons.

First, I'm getting sick of being grubby and working my ass off all the time. It's making me mentally and physically exhausted, and it isn't doing anything to make our attractive commander see me as a potential mate. Secondly, Kendra and I were outsiders among the

Draconians because we never dressed up or acted like queens. After careful consideration, I've decided to set a good example for my family. Most of them are younger and teens. I want them to fit in and feel included. I'll still work on my ship and wear a uniform when I work, but there's no need to dress like man all the damn time.

The trip to our ship doesn't take long, but I have to admit that seeing Earth growing smaller through the view screens that are shaped like small windows makes me feel some kind of way. Seeing my family distract the younger ones with the view of Earth and hearing them whispering among themselves is comforting. I've spent so long worrying about them that I don't know how to act, now that they're safe.

Although I'm dying for a good misting, I bounce out of the shuttle, intent on making sure every single member of my family is settled before taking a much-needed break. I've been sent a little map on my data pad showing they've created a little wing for us with twelve sleeping compartments. One by one, Tabor and I settle them all into their own rooms, showing them how things work and where to stow their few belongings. They're all fascinated with the misting units and the strange toilets that one straddles like a horse. I'm surprised they renovated the toilets so quickly. How is that even possible?

When finally Tabor opens the door to my own unit, I'm stunned. "This room is more spacious than the other suites." It's large and well appointed. The only thing out of place is a huge pallet-size crate that comes up to my shoulders. I can't deal with that right now.

"Since you are the queen in charge of this ship, we prioritize your comfort above all the others."

"That's really sweet. If you don't mind, I'm going to hit the mister and get ready to sleep. I feel like we've smashed about three days into one."

"I will make you a warm drink to help you relax."

"Thanks, I appreciate it." I whirl around and head for the cleanser before he can tell how happy I am to get some face-to-face time with him after my cleansing. That's the term warriors call misting themselves clean. I shut the door, pull off my clothes, and dump them into a nearby container that looks suspiciously like a hamper. The Draconians have special cabinets for soiled clothing that uses sonic waves to clean the fabric. I know for a fact we haven't had a chance to install anything like that yet.

Hopping into the mister, I let the warm mist envelope my body. I smell something that scents like flowers and follow my nose. It leads me to a good old-fashioned bar of soap. I haven't seen soap in two years and could only afford the cheap stuff before that. This is smooth, pink and smells like roses. I absolutely love roses. Suddenly, a bar of high class soap magically appearing in my cleansing unit becomes the biggest unsolved mystery of my life. I spend way too much time lathering my body and hair with the luxurious bar, temporarily forgetting the gorgeous dragon warrior waiting in my quarters.

When I finally force myself from the cleanser, I realize there is no mechanism to blow-dry my body. Since that's a standard feature of cleansing units, I assume it's simply another feature they haven't had time to install. I'm dripping all over the place, so I look around for something, anything to dry off with. It doesn't take me long to find big, thirsty towels, which I use to dry the leftover moisture from my body. I'm honestly feeling like the queen of the world right now, especially when I discover a long human-style robe folded up on a rack to the side. I must have missed that when I snatched the towels. The last sixteen hours might have been a complete roller-coaster, but it's turning into perfection. I finger comb my hair and head out to sample Tabor's idea of a relaxing drink.

I find him pulling small metal boxes from the ginormous crate and realize the larger one is merely filled with the small metal boxes from his shopping trip. He stops long enough to bring me the drink he promised. He then returns to rummaging through the boxes.

When I take the steaming cup from him, I realize how much I miss cup handles. "Are you moving in?" My question is asked as I gaze over my cup at him. His startle response is almost amusing. "You wish me to reside in here in your quarters?" Poor guy can't keep the shock out of his voice.

I respond with nod towards his huge crate. "Maybe. I only asked because you brought all your shopping with you."

A smile lights up his face. "The shopping is for you and your kin, my queen."

I jolt forward in my seat, almost spilling my beverage. "I don't have enough money to buy all this stuff."

"It is my honor to provide for your needs, my queen." His eyes land on me again and his expression can only be described as warm.

"Is this some kind of courting gesture?"

He stops rummaging, freezing into place. A long awkward silence spins out before he turns to face me. "Perhaps it would be if warriors were permitted to pursue queens. Since we are not, please know that I am proud to support you in any way you find acceptable."

I'm dumbfounded. "Where did you even get this much money?"

"Do you remember me at your side while you dug gemstone?"

"Yep, I remember you kept coming back to stoke our fire and see that we had food, clean water, and warm clothing. Your kindness is the only reason we were able to pull this plan off."

Rather than being happy about that comment, he looks dejected. "I wish only to serve."

Setting my drink down, I walk over to him. "I don't think that's entirely true. Maybe in the beginning that was the reason you looked out for us, but somewhere along the line things changed."

"Queens always seem to know what a warrior is thinking. It is an unfair advantage." His words may sound complaining but his voice tone is sad and dispirited.

I bring my hands up to cup his face and his eyes go wide. His wings release from the tight fold into a half-open fan on each side of his body. I can tell he's embarrassed by losing his wing control in front of me. I rub each cheek gently with my thumbs, keeping my voice soothing. "I left Earth two years ago, and we've known each other for most of that time. Being around you changed how I feel as well."

"You do not have to accept me merely because I am a good provider and protector. Any warrior would take you under his wing and treasure you for all times."

"What if I don't want to be under any other warrior's wing? I've only ever been under your wing, and I like it there."

His eyes grow warm and adoring again. Let's face it, warriors tend to school their expressions, but you can always tell by looking them in the eyes. "Say it clearly, so I know your mind, my queen. I do not wish to presume."

I wrap one hand around the back of his neck, barely able to reach it on my tiptoes and drag him down. Instead of a human kiss, I rub the side of my face up one side of his face and down the other, in a traditional Draconian kiss, before whispering softly in his ear. "I want you as my Takadon. What do you say? Are you up to having the queen everyone else thinks strange as your mate?"

"You are the only queen I have ever wished to make my own."

"Good, because I'm choosing you."

"We will take things slowly, so you can get used to having me around."

Giving him a tiny human kiss on the side of his mouth, I murmur, "Or maybe we can take things fast. It's not like we're strangers or anything."

He moves his face, clearly hoping to capture more of my kisses. He's adorable and I can't help but kiss a tiny trail down his chin to his neck. "I approve of fast only if it will not leave you regretting taking me to you," he says.

"I'm not one for regrets."

Uncertainty clouds his expression. "You have only smiled at me for a few days."

Turning his face to me, I try to make him understand. "I've been smiling at you in my heart for a very long time. I just couldn't allow myself to be distracted from rescuing my family."

"You intentionally kept your smile from me?"

"Yeah, I'm real sorry about that. Can you forgive me?"

He half-smiles down at me. "Queens do not ask forgiveness of warriors."

I almost laugh, cause he's making a joke for the first time ever with me. "In that case I demand that you forgive me for lusting after you all these months without letting you know."

"Your words provoke such a powerful feeling of possessiveness, that I wish to bar the door and stay sequestered with you for many months."

"You can't stay tonight. I just remembered we have to meet the Earth ambassador tomorrow."

He bites his lip before responding. "We would not make a good showing, swamped in my mating scent, my queen."

"I guess my idea of going fast isn't feasible right now. Darn, I was really looking forward to a little throw down, my new Takadon."

"It is enough to know that you lust after me, as I do you." He steps back, but the expression on his face tells me it's killing him. Suddenly, the warrior's mask has evaporated. It makes me wonder if I've finally broken through his emotional defenses, or the Draconian think it's inappropriate to withhold emotions from your mate. Either way it's nice to get that much closer to him. "I will busy myself with other duties until we meet with the ambassador, my queen."

"The minute we get back, you're going to lock is us in. Be sure the other warriors know you're going to be out of commission for a while."

"It will be my pleasure to tell them so. However, it would be best if you sent out a message to them yourself. Just post it on our main feed, and they will know it is true."

"I'm going to do that right now." Making the go away gesture, I keep my voice light and playful. "Now go, before I change my mind."

"All will be as you wish, my lovely and clever queen."

My head comes up hard and fast. No one has ever taken liberties with my queen title before. He just chuckles and strolls out the door. Hot damn, my guy's funny too! I'll add to the long list of qualities I adore about him. I get the sneaking suspicion, this queen thing is about to get interesting.

I'm kind of amazed that one truly awkward conversation got me the perfect man. I imagine our little ones with wings, flying away instead of running away when they're in trouble and almost laugh. I know he's no breeder, but between the two of us, we should be able to manage our own baseball team. It occurs to me to wonder if the Draconian have organized sports. Somehow, I doubt it. They seem overly serious and dedicated to their queens.

indness of Strangers

~ Tabor ~

Waking early, I realized that my life changed for the better last night. The queen of my deepest desire chose me from among all the other warriors to be her mate. Not only her mate, I am to be her Takadon, her first, foremost, and because she is human, her only mate. Tonight she will claim me as her own. The thought of our naked bodies rubbing together, her sweet kisses and the scent of her body in heat threatens to make me hard. I am no breeder, nor do I have young already to offer her, yet she chooses me. I know is partially because she finds me attractive, but she also sees my worth as a male. That means everything to me.

"Wake Takadon Tabor, there is work to be done."

I bolt up to a sitting position, my wings flailing about in a most undignified manner. Scarn, Timric and Phan are all squeezed into my tiny private sleeping quarters. Such privacy is the one luxury allocated to a commander, yet here they are.

My horns perk up as I struggle to get my wings under control.

"Why are you in my quarters?" You have never entered my space unannounced before." They're all staring at me with their warrior's face but beneath their matching stoic expressions there is amusement. I'm missing something but I cannot place quite what it is.

Straightening, I state clearly. "Get out. You should not be here."

Scarn laughs and tosses me a fresh uniform. I know immediately that something is amiss. This garment feels heavier than all the ones I have worn before. "Who redesigned our uniforms?"

Phan announces, "Only yours got redesigned. Queen Ella assisted Scarn in coming up with a new family symbol that represents the merging of our lines. Queen Kearney announced that you are her Takadon last night and we worked through the night to make sure you had a proper uniform to wear."

I blink at my proud brother. "What of you? Queen Kendra chose you as her Takadon. Where is your new uniform?"

"She can call me chosen all day long, but it is not so until I come into my hormones. Only then can I formally accept her offer of mating."

"Are you not upset by this turn of events?"

He shrugs. "She chose me and has elected to keep me. I am happy to be at her side and she never makes me feel that I am lacking. However, we are not here to talk about me. We wish to congratulate you for being selected as Queen Kearney's Takadon."

I begin unfolding the uniform and notice that it has red piping and a strange symbol of a dragon standing sideways. "Our new symbol has a dragon?"

Scarn answers gruffly, "It was on their family crest from olden times. It appears that ancient humans were acquainted with dragons, though it is not known how."

When I come to my feet, I can't stop smiling. "It is a strong design. I will wear it proudly." They take turns thumping me on the shoulder and congratulating me. Pride surges in my chest, not only to have been chosen but to have males who care about my happiness as friends. Then I realize how fruitful this mission has been. All of us have found the favor of a queen. Even Elder Scarn is often seen in the company of the queen mother, Ella. I'm certain that he never thought to find the favor of a queen, and he deserves all the happiness that such a lucky happenstance can bring.

Walking the corridors of our ship has new meaning for me. If my queen does not wish to live on our home world, we will raise our young on this ship. Both options appeal to me equally. I make my rounds to each station and then seek out Elder Scarn again to speak to him about creating a hatchery. My instinct is to visit my queen, but I am unsure if we could resist mating. Therefore I keep myself busy in other ways. Even though there are no infants, I wish us to have enough time to for the unit to be functional before our young begin arriving.

We begin working out a rough plan and assign warriors to begin working on the initial framework. I manage to keep myself busy for the better part of the morning before making my way to see my queen.

I find her in the company of her mother and sister queens. "Greetings my queen, I see you are ready for your meeting with the ambassador."

"The Strovians will meet us there. They're acting kind of uptight and it's causing me to wonder what their real motivation is in involving us in the meeting."

I turn the situation over in my mind. "Perhaps they hope to be seen in a better light by being introduced by a human." I feel nothing unusual about this meeting, but will take no risks with my queen. "Timric, you will accompany us. You will tell me if you sense trouble. Between your gift and my own, we can keep Queen Kearney safe."

"It is my honor to serve, Takadon Tabor."

I'm pleased to hear my new title on every warrior's lips. Perhaps that makes me vain or selfish, but it is true none the less. After careful consideration I believe it is because we have not mated. One we are one in that way, it will not matter to me what others say. Until then I will take solace in knowing she publicly claimed me.

"You look really nice in your new uniform." Her admiring eyes are eating me up from head to toe, lingering over my wings. I let them fall open a bit and she smiles. To know that my body pleases her fills me with pride and makes me brazen enough to chance a compliment of my own in front of others.

She's wearing a long red gown and has her hair styled on top of her head again. She's wearing a red belt of some shimmery fabric with a metal jewel-encrusted buckle with our new symbol stamped upon it. "You look beautiful in the gown I chose for you, though you appear no less fetching in a uniform, or, I suspect, devoid of all clothing."

Her mouth falls open at hearing my words, but she is pleased by my audacity. I am growing to learn that my queen greatly approves of forwardness in a male.

"We'll revisit this conversation after you've seen me devoid of clothing, my takadon. Now let us get moving. I have no intention of showing up late for our meeting." Stalking past me, she heads for the door.

We follow her to the loading bay, and when we enter the shuttle, I see she is bringing trade items. I wonder if she intends to trade for seeds or other items from her list while we are there. Perhaps she just wishes to trade for more luxury items. She motions for me to sit beside her and clasps my hand. Her hands are soft and warm, reminding me how very little she resembles Draconian queens. They have claws and little patience for the needs of a warrior.

"I've been thinking about this situation with the Strovian. If they're here to trade for brides, helping other ships come to Earth would be in their interest, especially if we make a deal to use their bubble to get back. The ships that came here will probably be full of women, how do we know they won't just jump us to their home world, keep all the women and enslave the males?"

Rubbing my chin thoughtfully, I am forced to admit that my

queen has a point. "Just because we have not heard of them performing evil deeds, it does not mean they are honest in their dealings with other species."

"I'm not trying to be paranoid or anything. It's just that we've done the impossible by just making it back to Earth. I don't want all our hard work and planning to land my family in an even worse situation than they were in already."

I place my free hand over our joined hands and squeeze slightly. "You are wise to think of this. We know nothing of the Strovians except that they have never made war with us. If you feel it is safer we can fly back under our own power."

"Let's meet with them face-to-face and see if we can get a read on how trustworthy they are."

Our conversation puts the other warriors on high alert. They signal our ship to raise shields and remain alert. Suddenly, fifty warriors do not seem like enough to protect so many queens.

When we land on the ambassador's office landing pad, we see the Strovian ship waiting for our arrival. We exit the ship and as the Strovian delegation moves forward, I notice they are dressed differently from their normal traders. They are not even wearing the uniforms of their world. The Strovians are one of the stranger aliens I've seen. They are pale blue with skinny bodies, long spindly arms that fold up double, meaning they actually walk on their knees to speak face-to-face with humanoids. Their posture is too jerky and aggressive for this situation. Leaning over, I whisper, "They are not official representatives from Strovia Prime. My best guess is they are usurpers, gone rogue or have founded another planet."

"I hope it's the last item on your list of explanations, cause I certainly don't want to end up in the middle of a Strovian civil war."

"Be cautious in your introductions, my precious queen."

When we sit at a large oval table in the main conference room, the ambassador is already there waiting for us. He stands to welcome us, extending his hand. I reach out to shake his hand as he speaks. "Welcome, Queen Kearney and Commander Tabor. We were pleased to get your message requesting a meeting."

"Thank you for seeing us, Ambassador Tham. I apologize for the short notice." Glancing down at my handheld, I reply smoothly, "If you don't mind, I'd like to take an opportunity to introduce L'tam De Artor, Captain of the trade ship Darnovo."

"Please be seated. What can I do for you today?"

Artor begins speaking immediately. "I wish to negotiate a trade contract with Earth."

The ambassador leans back and arcs his fingers together. It's the typical supervillain pose, but on the gray-haired older man it just looks like he's being pensive. "Earth already has a trade deal in place with your people, Captain Artor. I negotiated it myself."

"There has been a civil disagreement with our world, leading to a division of sorts. We wish our own contract negotiations."

"I've been apprised of your situation by the Strovian ambassador. It seems the split was over allocation of brides. Strovia Prime allows brides to choose their own husbands, but your group thought that wasn't fair to the some of the males."

"The Strovian elite are so blinded by their desire for delicate human brides, they will refuse them nothing. We simply wish a fair system where males are assigned brides at random."

My queen's head whips around, and her outraged words are nothing the Strovian captain wishes to hear. "Are you telling me that I've gone out of my way to introduce you, and you want to treat human women like meat? Have you no morals? Assigning a woman to be someone's husband isn't going to make anyone happy, least of all the man she's being forced to marry."

"We made a deal. You were to stand with me during this meeting."

"The deal we made was for me to introduce you, nothing more."

As he shifts forward in his seat, Artor's voice turns low and malicious. "Your cooperation was implied. Why else would I need you to set up the meeting?"

"I've got records of our transaction. You've had your introduction. Perhaps it is best if you leave."

The ambassador speaks. "I will permit you to operate under the current contract. However, the women have a list of rights included in the contract. One of which protects their right to choose. If I find that you have violated any of the rules, even once, you will not be allowed to trade with Earth in the future. Am I making myself clear?"

"Yes, ambassador. We are not renegades. Therefore, we respect the law."

I get a feeling in the pit of my stomach that he is lying because I sense danger. I glance at Timric and the young warrior gives a slight shake of his head to indicate this is not right.

"I will speak on behalf of our ship and queens. Do not approach our queens and do not interfere with our activities on this planet. We will take whatever steps necessary to protect our queens."

L'tam De Artor leaps from his seat and moves around closer to our delegation. Timric is closer, so he steps in front of the ungainly alien. Issuing a soft warning, he slowly brings his hand to rest on his weapon. "Stop where you are. I don't wish you to be any closer to my queen."

"I care nothing for your human bride." When he shoots our queen a glance, everyone in the room knows he's lying. His gaze is quick but filled with depraved hunger. I can't stand his eyes on my queen. The feeling of danger is so strong, it's swamping every other emotion. I'm on my feet before I can stop myself, moving toward him.

The ambassador stands abruptly, and his voice stops me in my tracks. "Your audience is over, Captain Artor. I will give you one day to make your trades, but after that you are to leave our airspace."

He staggers back a step and his chin comes up. "As you wish,

ALIEN COMMANDERS RELUCTANT BRIDE

ambassador. You will see that we are beings who are willing to follow the rules."

Captain Artor's behavior swings from controlled to aggressive and back again so quickly, that I know he can't possibly be in full control of his emotions. That makes him unpredictable, which in turn makes him dangerous. The Strovian delegation takes their leave with the little dignity they can muster, and I'm about to breathe easy again.

My Kearney lets out a sigh of her own before speaking. "That was all kinds of weird."

The ambassador gestures for us to sit again. Folding his hands in his lap when he sits, he allows his wrinkled face to settle into a frown. "I'm sorry you had to be witness to that display of depravity. Rest assured that Earth Gov is not happy to be forced into trading willing brides to care for the multitude that remains behind on our dying world. Rest assured, we do hold those who trade for brides to their contract. I wish it weren't necessary to barter in women this way, but if we are to survive, we must."

I quickly interject. "There are very few habitable worlds to be had, ambassador."

"It's unfortunate that we spoiled our own planet. That's not anybody's fault but our own."

My queen seems broken-hearted with the whole situation. "Even if we found a habitable world, the logistics of transferring everyone and building housing would be a herculean task."

"Earth Gov wanted me to communicate to you that the Draconian atmospheric cleanser is slowly tilting our environment back into balance. We appreciate your assistance."

I dip my head respectfully. "I assisted with the construction of the device on my home world. It took us many months to calibrate it properly. I am pleased that my brethren got it into proper placement in your atmosphere."

"Since your people don't trade in brides, I was wondering what brought you to Earth."

"My sister and I signed up for the bride's registry and our ship was attacked. We ended up on the new Draconian home world."

"I wonder why your people never use the proper name for your world. Onello is a lovely name."

I speak up, "The queen who rules our world chose it because it reminded her of an ancient hero in Earth mythology. It is very near the Draconian word for fecal matter. That is the reason our warriors shun the name. I believe our queens model their behavior off our reluctance to speak the word."

The ambassador bursts out laughing. Even my lovely queen is smiling. For the first time I see the humor in our situation. "I do not believe even her mate would enlighten her about this, as it would be considered rude to embarrass a queen."

"I'm glad you told me this, Commander. It helps me understand your customs but not why you have come."

"I bought a ship and came back to check on my family. They aren't doing well since my father passed. We invited them to our new home world and they were grateful for the offer. We brought them up to my ship last night."

"You are a kind person to have come back for them. I wonder if I could press you for a favor."

"I'd be happy to do anything I can for Earth Gov, ambassador."

"Our church has been sheltering a small group of children for years. The poor innocent souls lost their parents or were turned out to rely upon the kindness of strangers. We gathered them from here and there, shepherding and guiding them. We thought for sure that we'd be able to find jobs for them."

"They are all grown now and there are few jobs to be had. We don't want to just turn them out to fend for themselves. However, things being what they are here on Earth, we find that we aren't in a position to take more vulnerable children until we determine what to do with the adults. We simply can't afford to keep both, nor do we have the space to house them."

My queen asks quietly, "How many are in need of shelter?"

"We currently have sixty in our care."

"Shall I assume all are female?"

The older man wrung his hands anxiously. "Forty-six are adult females, three are adult males and one is an intellectually disabled female. If you can't see fit to find her a suitable situation, we would be willing to keep Jenny."

I feel compelled to speak on this vulnerable queen's behalf. "Our medical skills are quite advanced. If we cannot do anything to help with her disability, I feel certain she would be welcome in the queen housing."

"I'm not sure I understand what that is. I hope you aren't suggesting a brothel or anything like that."

Queen Kearney jumps into the conversation again. "The warriors would probably kill anyone who suggested creating a brothel on our new home world. The queen housing is a really nice apartment-style complex that was built to the standards the warriors thought was appropriate for a female. Trust me when I say they spared no expense."

"Is proper security in place?"

"No and yes. As best I can tell, there's no crime on our home world. Therefore there is no need for security. The warriors think of security as something that's necessary when a woman comes into contact with the outside world."

"Are you saying a warrior would never take liberties with a woman?"

"Well, sure they would, if and only if the woman invited them. They're "No means no" fanatics."

I state emphatically, "The punishment for pressing oneself upon a queen is death."

"Yep, that's how it works. They make no bones about the fact that anyone who harms a queen on a ship gets vented into space. I never even considered what they'd do to a warrior who stepped out of line that way on our world because it's literally never happened. If a woman doesn't find a guy she wants, they'll hook her up with any other species she wants or even bring her back to Earth. I should mention that they won't let us hang around forever without selecting a mate, but they're not pressuring anyone either. I've been with them almost two years, and I just picked my mate yesterday."

"That sounds like possibly the best situation for women that I've heard of out of all the different species who come here looking for brides. Would it be possible for me to have a look at your ship myself and talk to the other members of your family?"

"Of course, you are welcome to visit my ship anytime we're in orbit. Of course if we end up relocating the group you spoke of, we'll need to lay in more provisions."

"I'm afraid we have a very limited budget, but I will try to ensure…"

"I brought some gemstone and other trade items. I was hoping to trade for seeds and household goods for our family units back home. Do you think we could work together to see both are needs are met?"

"I have been given leave to do whatever is necessary to see our charges are well situated. We have several universities with seed banks. I feel certain they would be willing to donate seeds. We are unable to use most of our seeds because of environmental concerns make traditional outdoor growing nearly impossible in most places on Earth."

"Are you certain your charges are willing to relocate to an alien world?"

"I fear they have little choice, but they will all go willingly or not at all."

My queen tapped her fingers on the table quietly as if she were mulling over something of great importance. "I would be willing to take the women if each will take care of a homeless child on the voyage from Earth to our new home world. I feel certain that I can find good homes for them with caring human mothers. That might give your charity a bit of time to regroup before taking on more children."

"I would be a fool to turn down such an offer. The truth is your world is the only one I feel remotely comfortable with taking our innocents. I must warn you that our church elders will expect to have regular supervision with them until we know for sure they are safe and well cared for on your world."

"I can't imagine a problem with that. The space communication relay system is in place and functioning properly, so getting a real time signal should be no problem."

"Then it is agreed."

hicken Plucking

~ Kearney ~

My mother screeches, "You have how many coming?" The poor woman's eyes are threatening to pop right out of her head. She was all for us taking some church-sheltered, vulnerable women. It's been almost a week, and I've been putting off telling her the actual number, for just this reason. She was fine with the plan, right up until she learned the number.

Unfortunately the number seventy-four blew her mind. It's a number that will go down in infamy. Okay, maybe I've been a bit ambitious, but I can't stand thinking of them being turned out. At least we had land and shelter. They would be bunking out in the lower level of the bio dome, where all the really evil shit goes down.

"I'm sick and tired of human women always getting the shaft. How the heck do you think they're going to survive in the under-world of the bio dome after being raised in a church?"

"The ship might be huge but over half of it's not even been made habitable."

"We didn't anticipate needing the space for a while, so we cleared the rooms and created a renovation schedule.

"That's all well and good but where are we going to put them, Keary?"

I reply absently, "We'll have to double up or something." Looking up to catch her eye, I explain, "Tabor's working on a plan right now. My big problem is I haven't been able to find Virgil, and I owe him a water purifier. I promised that I'd get it to him the day after he landed. I had to leave it with the local mail center."

I can tell she doesn't want to talk about that man who forced her to sign over her property. She's still intent on getting me to see reason about the number of people making the voyage back to our home world. "Virgil's clan is thirty strong. You do know that, don't you?"

A little quick math tells me that with our family numbering about twenty-five, the Grayson clan being thirty, the orphans being seventy-four and the warriors being fifty that means our ship will be carrying around a hundred and eighty people. Suddenly, the vein in my temple is throbbing like it has a heartbeat of its own. I rub it with a vengeance, hoping to make it calm down a bit.

Tabor looks up from his data pad. He's been a good sport about the whole situation, considering we still haven't gotten a chance to consummate our bond. I felt so old using that term. He looks up at me wearing the strange virtual reality goggles he uses to link into the ship's mainframe. His dark eyes look huge but pleased.

"I am close to a solution. We can move all the warriors to the loading bay. We are used to sleeping rough and even with it loaded down cargo, it is still spacious enough to accommodate our numbers. At any given time a third of us will be on duty and that cuts down on the space we need."

"Don't use the word we when talking about where warriors will sleep, cause you are going to be bunking with me."

He smiles, quickly dipping his head. "Thank you, my queen. We have renovated a large dormitory and about thirty chambers at this point, not counting the fifteen rooms your family occupies. We can probably get at least twenty more rooms renovated and worthy of a queen prior to leaving this world."

My mother chimes in, "They don't need to be worthy of a queen. They just need to be clean basic living."

"As you wish, queen mother."

"Sorry Tabor, I'm not trying to be pushy. I just want everyone sorted into a reasonably appropriate room. We can share cleansing rooms."

Tabor's head jerks up to look at her. I interject soothingly, "We're used to having one or two cleansing rooms per house. I promise, nobody's going to lose their mind over sharing."

"If we create a cleansing room between each room, we can perhaps have thirty additional rooms ready."

"How many is that total?"

"The dormitory can comfortably hold fifty people. That leaves about thirty rooms. You and Kendra will want private rooms. The queen mother will wish a room for her and the twins."

"Put Scarn in my room. He's helpful with the little ones and a good bed warmer."

Tabor ducks his head again but I see the pleased look on his face. "Scarn is one of our most respected elders. You will not regret taking him to you, queen mother."

"I don't imagine I will, but thanks for talking him up to me. He'll be pleased to hear you think so well of him. Now, I think we should turn the dorm into a nursery and keep all the kids together. Everyone can take turns looking out for the little ones."

I point out the obvious. "They'll get more quality time with an adult if we assign them to the older and more responsible women to care for."

My mother puts her hands on her hips and gives me a meaningful look. "Sure they will, but they also might get attached to their caregivers. It's not fair to put that kind of burden on these women or for the little ones to end up disappointed when they get placed with another family. It's better to bed them all down in one common space and tell them they're going to live with their forever families."

I have to admit that I didn't think of all that. "I can't believe you came up with all that on the fly. I used to think you were the smartest women in the universe, and now you've just proved it true."

My mother tosses me an amused smirk. "You don't have to lay it on quite so thick, Keary. You know I'll do what I can to make this work."

"It looks like we've got our work cut out for us. According to my calculations we will have enough rooms to put 2-3 women to a room. The men are going into the loading bay with the warriors. If that's not okay with them, they can stay behind."

My mother rolls her eyes, "We put Virgil, Donna and their two little ones in one room and the same with Virgil's married sons. That way we're actually saving space in the long run."

I tease her playfully, "Hey, who's plucking this chicken anyway?"

"It looks like it's going to take all of us plucking at the speed of light to work our way out of this situation."

I have to laugh. "You might just be right about that."

Our conversation is interrupted by the arrival of the ambassador's shuttle. The plan was for him to visit first, look over the place and talk to my family. However, when word got out that we were prepared to find homes for the little ones, every elder in the church wanted to visit. My mother and Elder Scarn will be joining the tour. I figured elders talking to elders might smooth the way. If they don't want to risk the little ones, that's fine too. I'm just trying to do a good deed.

We hustle to the loading bay to meet them. Though I'm expecting some uptight men in suits, they're mostly women, and though they look really nice, they aren't what you would call dressed up. Looking down at my gown, I realize that I'm the one who's technically overdressed for the occasion. It's not a cringe-worthy misstep in a situation like this but it feels weird none the less.

The ambassador introduces the church elders. They're all around my mother's age, and I don't consider that old, but who am I to question their ways? We hand off the tour to my mother and Elder Scarn after the first hour or so and head back to my quarters for some rest and relaxation.

Scooting over towards Tabor, I announce. "We're getting a lot done in a day."

"You are a very productive queen. I have noticed this over the last couple of solars. You dug gemstone like a droid set on its highest setting and got all your warriors lined up for this mission with supreme efficiency. If I had not gotten stung, we would have still had three or four lunars of travel before reaching Earth."

"Hey, you're right about that. Catching a ride with space folding crazy Strovian only happened because our repairs were delayed. I hated to see you down that way. Phan said it was touch and go there for a bit because the poison got into your bloodstream."

"I did not know that. I'm glad I survived. If not, you might have ended up with a less worthy mate." My hot warrior looks all kinds of smug as he wraps his wing around me and pulls me closer.

"I can't believe I once thought you had no sense of humor."

His eyes fill with pain. "Before you came into my life, I'm not certain I had much of a sense of humor. Then again, perhaps it was just a different type of humor."

"Well you're all kinds of sexy and funny now."

"Is this some kind of secret queen code for you wish to mate with me now? If so I am ready. In fact, I am more than ready. I mean to say, I wish to join with you."

"Aw, you're cute when you're babbling. Just so you know, I'm right there with you."

"I wish to learn the human kiss, so I might please you, and in doing so seal you to me."

"You don't have to make up reasons to kiss, handsome. I'm willing to cuddle up and kiss you every chance we get."

"I wish that I had known this before now. You and I need more accurate communication, my sweet and accommodating queen."

I drag him down for a kiss, beginning by ghosting my lips over his. His eagerness is charming the pants off me, or the gown in my case. Wings flutter up around me and he pulls me on top of his body. I go willingly, straddling his lap. I love the feel of his soft wings pressing me into his hard body. Slowly he goes from novice to groping insecure learner to master. It's not occurred to him to use his tongue but this smokin' hot warrior can kiss like nobody's business. The moment I relay into the spell of seduction he's weaving, we get a buzz on our com.

Tabor's deep, sexy voice prompts the com unit. "Speak. We are listening." His hands smother over my body, exploring and teasing my tender bits.

I'm totally distracted, and vaguely think his response to the prompt is the Draconian version of a hello.

Virgil's face comes up on the com, and he looks like death warmed over. He's covered in filth, and his hair is kind of wild. Before we can speak, he launches into a breathless speech. "We had a wild fire at our place a couple of days after we met. It swept through our property and drove us up the mountain. Everything's so brittle since the fall that it just went up in flames."

"Did you lose anyone?"

"Thank God no, but several are injured. We didn't have any way to contact you, and then I realized that if you couldn't get ahold of me, you would leave the purifier at the mail center. Though they no longer deliver mail, it's practically the only place you could leave something for me. Thank you for attaching the communication unit."

"Are you in town right now? We'll come for you immediately."

"Yes, we're in town. We lost everything, though."

"You must be starving. Go to the Sportsman's Paradise and

order whatever you want. I'll be there within the hour to pay for it and pick you all up."

"Thanks Keary girl, I knew you'd keep your word to us." He looks relieved and like I just saved the life of all his family. Though that's not far from the truth, I don't feel like it's anything amazing. I feel like humans are mostly all on Team Poverty at this point. Teamworking solutions is the only course of action that makes sense. I got a chance at a better life, and I'll make sure to pay it forward to as many people as I can.

I sure am disappointed about once again having sex with my hot new Takadon bumped off my schedule. I try to act like my sex isn't a hot throbbing mess for him. It's best to keep things light and move on before I cry my eyes out. "So much for fancy gowns and hot sex tonight. I'll get changed, and we can grab a shuttle."

"I will com the loading bay and have it prepped and waiting for us."

"I'm sorry we can't ever seem to catch a break."

"Warriors are accustomed to putting the safety of others before all else. There are queens and young ones in need of our help. I will set my own needs aside for them." His expression slips back to protector mode and he adds, "That does not mean I am pleased to be disrupted with my queen."

"Me either. You and I have a lifetime to spend together. What difference will a few more hours make?"

"I hope none. My cock says he will perish if he is not inside you soon. I thought it proper to pass along the message in time to save his life."

I can't help the laughter that spills from my mouth. "We wouldn't want anything to happen to my favorite body part, now would we?"

He takes a step closer. "So, we are choosing favorite body parts now?"

Pointing towards the door, I say sternly, "Out, you devilishly sexy man. You have no idea how close I am to losing my battle to do the right thing here."

Tucking his wings neatly behind him, he takes a dramatic step backwards. "In that case, I will tempt you no more."

He doesn't leave, so I do. I feel like I should grab a quick misting but there's simply no time. So, instead I pull off the gown and put on a crisp clean uniform. I grab my utility belt and boots and slide them on as I make my way back into the common room. Tabor is standing near the open door, so we make a run for the loading bay double quick.

Literally everything is my life moves at the speed of light. I feel like a ball rolling from one crisis to another. I really need some control over my life, and the only way to get it is to keep working my way through the tangle of problems until we get to the end.

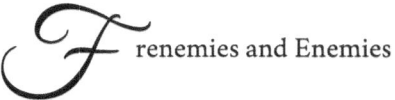 renemies and Enemies

~ Tabor ~

I have a beautiful mate who desires to mate with me. She makes jest with me about all the things that are difficult in our life. Her playful and positive attitude takes the sting out of even our worst day. I would never put my pleasure before the lives of people in need. The only positive aspect to this situation that I can think of is the longer we delay joining, the more intense the experience will be.

I have never known the touch of a female before being chosen by my sweet mate. I wonder what her pale soft form looks like and how it will feel when our skin touches. I've felt a fierce loyalty and admiration building in my chest for her over the last couple of solars, but this new feeling of need growing in my gut is fiercer still. I will never take being at her side for granted. She will be my everything until we are old and her hair turns white. Eventually, my wings will droop and I will lose my strength. Somehow I know deep down inside that she will still stand by and think no less of me. I will become an elder, valued for my wisdom.

Seeing her weaving between tables, talking and passing more food to the clan who are both friends and enemies, I see her devotion to her people. I admire so many things about my queen that I cannot begin to name them all. I reach over and order more food to take with us, because I feel there is always need for delicious Earth food when we have so many humans about. I wonder about hiring on human cooks to keep the kind of food our queens like fresh and available. I send out a message to the general posting on this world for cooks willing to work on a Draconian ship. I begin to get replies right away.

Suddenly, a large man is standing over me. "You want a cook. I'm a cook. Hire me." He's wearing white and has his arms crossed over his chest with a cooking implement in one hand. He is older but seems as capable as any of his kind.

"Sit and we will talk."

He drops down into the chair in front of me with a little more attitude than seems prudent for the situation. I try to explain my thoughts about having a cook on board. "As you read in my message, my name is Tabor. I am Takadon to Queen Kearney."

"I am Samuel Patterson. People call me Sam."

"I am pleased to meet you, Sam. We have many human females on our ship. We would like to hire someone to cook for us full time so they can have their choice of foods. Are you willing to work aboard a trade ship?"

"Yes."

"Do you work at this establishment full time?"

"I have worked here for ten years. All the others answer to me. I am head cook."

"You can make every food served on the menu at this eating place?"

"Of course. I teach others to cook as well."

We are shooting questions and answers back and forth rapidly with very little small talk. This is my preference, but I did not think humans acted like warriors. "I do not know how much cooks earn."

One side of his mouth tilts up. "We make a million kabillion dollars a year, and we get paid in advance."

Reaching to the side of my belt, I pull out a small bag of gemstone. "I do not think that is correct information, but will this be enough for you to get cooking utensils and enough food for a six-month voyage? We have a hydroponics bay so we will be growing most of our own green food."

He scarfs it up from the table and pulls the bag open, peering inside. "I do not know. Maybe it will be enough."

Frowning, I pull a second pouch out and lay it before him. "This should certainly be enough. You will be feeding about a hundred and eighty people a day. If you need assistants you have my leave to hire them." Giving him a stern look, I explain. "My queen intends to become a proper trader, so we are looking for someone willing to make a solid, long-term commitment. We'll stay on our new home world between trade runs. I will see that you and your crew have a place to stay there."

"I have a family. They will come with me. The other cooks might have family as well."

"I'll see to your accommodations myself. Use some from the gemstone allotment to purchase household items, for we are carrying more queens than we expected, so we have little to spare. Can you tell me how many assistants you will hire? I need to have my crew prepare quarters for them."

"I will need at least four. They will expect private rooms. When do you want us to be ready by?"

"Be ready as soon as possible. We hope to begin our journey within the next week. If you can come earlier to set up your cooking space, I will pay you another pouch of gemstone."

I will message you when we are ready,"

"I must give you a final word of warning, Sam. Do not bring people who will upset our queens or cause chaos on our ship. The penalty for harming a queen is death among our people. All the females are to be respected at all times."

"Even my female?"

"Every female is to be cherished and protected. Any who touch your female will end up vented into space. We have no jail or time to waste with males who hurt females."

"We are of the same mind. I will see you in two days' time." Standing, he held his hand out in the strange human custom of shaking. No one has ever tried to shake my hand before but I have seen it done. I place my palm in his and he moves his hand up and down. Before I can blink he's gone. This human moves fast for one so large.

My sweet queen sits across from me and pushes a drink my way. "What was that all about?"

"I secured a cook to make human food."

"Wow, that's so nice. Wait, did he sign on as crew?"

"I nod. Our queens should not be forced to eat food bars or the food a warrior makes."

"I'll tell you a little secret, handsome."

I lean over to hear this secret, curious about what she is thinking.

"The more people we can get off this rock the better in my opinion. So I say good job. How much is he charging us?"

"So far, only two bags of gemstone, though I did promise him a bonus bag if he stocked the kitchen with food and cooking implements."

"You got robbed, hot stuff. It doesn't matter. We've got enough gemstone for something this important."

"I did not think you would see this as an important expenditure. Therefore, I spent my own gemstone."

She leans over and drops a chaste kiss on my lips. "It's important because we'll have children along on this voyage. They're notoriously picky eaters. Do you know human children will sometimes starve themselves rather than eat unfamiliar food?"

Shock tears though me at the thought of children being unable to tolerate our food. "No, this I did not know. I will message him right away that we have children that need fed."

"Thanks for looking out for us, handsome. Between the two of us, I'm beginning to think we can do anything."

As I look around at the people we have to come to help, I begin to see that my queen is right. It seems that when we work together, none can stand against us. Yet, it seems that everything is moving forward on his human world so fast that none of us can be certain our course is true.

This is about the time I notice not all the people dining in this establishment are human. I spy the one male I want nowhere near my queen. The Strovian, L'tam De Artor is sitting with a group of human traders. My ire is piqued when I realize his attention is on the queens in our group rather than his own business. I glare at him with as much malice as I can force into my expression, but he does not notice. The unstable male is far too focused on the young queen who happens to be sitting near him. I stand to interrupt his wandering eye, when I realize that beings are allowed to look at other beings on this world. I'm sure the humans have some law that precludes me from removing the offending male's eyes.

Thankfully, the Grayson clade appears to be finished with their food and the extras I ordered arrive, packed neatly in containers. I make haste to get my group moving towards the door. It seems my irritation knows no bounds when he stands to leave as well. I wish I could call my shuttle to land right in the middle of the bio dome but that is prohibited. Therefore, Artor gets to walk along side of us to the front exit. He's brazen as any male I've ever known, talking to our queens and pretending to be charming. I hate it when villains disguise themselves as warriors of worth. I keep my queen tucked under my wing and my eye on the Strovian and his crew.

The small beauty tucked under my arm tugs on my uniform. "Calm down. You're getting wound pretty tight over Captain Artor.

He's not done anything out of the way, so Earth Gov won't look kindly on you tearing his head off."

Again my smart and beautiful queen uses to jest to artfully navigate this stressful situation. She disarms me with a few words, a bit of understanding and a sweet smile. Though I am able to calm myself an infinitesimal bit, I do not take my eye off the object of my frustration.

Pulling her close, I human kiss the top of her head and whisper reassurances. "Though I sense great danger at this moment, I will control my urge to separate him from your kin."

The walk to the front exit is uneventful. However, when we separate to board our separate shuttles, Artor's eyes find mine. I freeze in mid step. The look on his face is a one of unmitigated glee. I look around, trying to figure out why he is so smug. I see nothing and this seems to please him even more. The sense of danger is so strong that I can almost taste it. I wish Timric were here with us. Perhaps he could better discern where the danger lies.

I insist the shuttle be inspected prior to lift off, but we find nothing alarming in our search. Kearney pats my chest and encourages me to lift off. Against my better judgement, I give the order to make for our ship.

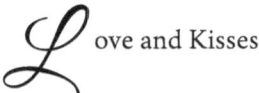ove and Kisses

~ Kearney ~

Finally all my family and the Grayson clan are safely on board our ship. The church elders accepted our offer of relocating their charges and the children needing homes. I think at the end of the day, they couldn't deny them the opportunity to relocate to a pristine new home world, and they had enough trust in us to keep them safe. We're all just trying to save as many as we can. That's the bottom line.

Tabor has been a real mess since we got back. He's acting like we brought a ticking time bomb back with us. He's got no call to be so paranoid. Virgil may be a gigantic ass in a lot of ways, but he'd never do anything to sabotage the ship or hurt anyone. It's all good because I'm about to distract him by using my womanly wiles.

He's pacing back and forth in my quarters. So I grab his hand and pull him over to the settee. It's an alien version of a sofa, except it doesn't have a back. Though no one's ever said, I think it doesn't have a back so their wings don't get crushed.

"Come sit with me. Your queen needs attending to. We're having our little throw down now, and if another emergency pops up, Scarn and my mother will have to deal with it."

He comes willingly, and I can tell he's slowly switching gears, becoming less paranoid and more aroused. He drops into the seat, clearly expecting me to sit on his lap like before. Instead I step back. His response is immediate. "What can I do to earn the favor of your touch, my queen?"

I slide my hands up to my throat, gently tugging open the magnetic seal on my uniform. "I have a word of advice for you, my takadon." I pull the seal open, exposing the fact that I didn't wear underwear today. His wings click open and I can't help but smile at his loss of control. "You might not want to bargain for the things you can have for free." I peel the top of the uniform from my body and shove it right down my thighs.

Tabor stares at me with his mouth hanging open for about three seconds and then he's on me so fast that I can't think of what to say. When a hot guy tosses you over his shoulder and heads for the bed, you're supposed to say something clever, but I got nothing. The way his dark eyes darkened yet again with lust literally took my breath away. My uniform is still down around my ankles, cause I didn't remove my boots before I tried to be all trampy and sexy.

He lays me gently on the bed and squats on the floor in front of me. His expression is all want but he takes his hands off me and holds them palms out. "I did not mean to over step my bounds with a queen."

I reach out and cup his chin with one hand. "Oh, you didn't overstep. Human women like males to take charge when it comes to mating."

"Explain this take charge." He is so serious, and I know it's because he's never been with a woman and is looking for me to set boundaries.

"I would be all kinds of thrilled if you explored my body. It's a great way to learn what I like. You're really smart so you'll be able to tell by my reactions what excites me. I'll tell you immediately if you do anything I don't like. I have to get really excited for the sex between us to be good. If you go slowly, you can have me any way you want. Does that make sense?"

"Yes." His voice sounds rough and almost inhuman. Logically, I know he's not human. Yet, sometimes I totally forget, because to me he's just the man I love.

I smile encouragingly. "My body is made to stretch. As long as you don't use your full strength against me, I won't break. I want your touch and give you full approval to do whatever you like with me."

His tongue comes out to run along his bottom lip, and his hands come out slowly to grasp the uniform around my ankles and tugs with one hand, while removing my boots one at a time with the other hand. His eyes zero in on my sex, and I know he wants me to open my legs. He doesn't say anything, so I drop him a clue. "You can demand I do things when we're intimate. If you do, I promise to obey."

"Spread your legs. I wish to see all the gods have given you." Again, something about his deep voice has me dropping my legs open almost immediately. "You have the same delicate strands on your sexy as you do on your head."

Maybe for him it's an idle observation, but for me it's embarrassing. "I normally shave it off, but I've had more important things to worry about lately. I didn't think you would want to examine my queenly parts quite so closely."

A smile flashes across his face. He thinks calling my pussy queenly is funny. A strong scent reaches my nostrils. It smells like musk, old leather, and hot sexy male. I find myself sucking in a lungful of it before I even realize what I'm doing. "You smell nice, my takadon."

I can't quite describe his pleasure at being called by that title, but I can see it on his face and his chest puffs up with pride each time I use it. This time, he also reaches out to run the backs of two fingers over my mound, toying with the triangle of soft curls. The next words out of his mouth blow me away.

"I like that you enjoy my mating scent, but know this. Every tiny strand growing here now belongs to me, and you will not remove any of it."

Shifting my legs, I wiggle with pleasure. "Yes, sir."

"What is this 'sir'? The language program does not translate it well."

"Sir is an honorarium we use for males. When a woman says it during intimacy it means she submits to the male's authority."

"I like this sir word. I wish to use if often when we're together." The sentence kind of trails off towards the end because he gets distracted tracing his finger up and down my body. I suck in a sharp breath when he circles one breast. I never knew the under-side of my breast was so sensitive. I state breathlessly, "You're supposed to take off your clothing as well."

His hand freezes, and he glances up to catch my eye. "Seeing me without clothing would be arousing for you, would it not?"

"If you only knew how many nights I thought about your body, you wouldn't need to ask that question."

Coming to his feet, Tabor pulls roughly on his uniform and is naked within seconds. Rather than appearing embarrassed or unsure of himself, he stands with his hands on his hips and flares his wings out. I have to admit, he is the most attractive man I've ever seen. Besides the miles and miles of gorgeous muscles, he has those dark brooding eyes and a somewhat more human face than most of the other warriors. He's just straight-up handsome. I notice his horns are throbbing slightly. Another woman might find that off-putting, but it just makes me want to handle them. An image of holding his horns while he licks my pussy pops into my mind. It makes me throb with lust.

My eyes travel over his body, landing on his long thick cock. He's so hard it practically plastered to his stomach. When he kneels between my legs, I'm more excited than I've ever been in my whole life. I probably should tell him this is my first time, but since it's likely his first time as well, it seems like unnecessary conversation. We've both had the same problem getting laid. There were practically no available men on Earth and everyone is aware that most Draconian males never got sex since there were usually a thousand warriors and one queen on their ships.

A huge hand comes up and cups my shoulder and the other lands on my hip. I stare at him wide-eyed as he drags my body down to the edge of the bed. When he leans over me, all I see is broad shoulders and horns. I must be the naughtiest woman in the 'verse, cause it flips all the right switches, sending my body into overdrive.

"Do not fear me." That's the last thing I hear before he leans over me and seals his lips to mine. I'm on sensory overload when his skin slides over mine, making my nipples draw into sharp points. I should have known my guy wouldn't let something like that slip his notice. Pulling back slightly, he inspects my breasts before cupping one in his hand and squeezing slightly. When he swirls his tongue around the tip I writhe beneath him. "You are small, and you move around when you're excited."

"Get back to work, you chatty devil." My voice sounds eager and needy, even to my own ears. Much to my absolute amazement, he does just as I ask. His hands wander over my body as his mouth teases one nipple then the other until I'm keening with need. Only then does he kiss his way down to my belly button. I remember he doesn't have one, cause he was hatched from a shell. He seems thoroughly fascinated by mine though. He fingers it, swirls his tongue inside and then licks me over and over, until I push his head down a bit. I know, that's really brazen, but I ache for him.

To be honest, he seems just as eager to explore my girly bits, first by sliding his fingers through my folds, then testing every square inch with his tongue. I wrap a hand around each horn and do a little exploring of my own. His big body jerks beneath me, and he begins tonguing me frantically. Ah, I've found his sweet spot. I tenderly run my hands up and down the length of his horns, they pull forward slightly and seem to vibrate against my palms. He moves his head to get a harder rub. I'm beginning to get overwhelmed with all the different sensations and jolts of pleasure.

When the talented man's tongue finds my clit, it's game over. I'm strung so tight that I come the minute he begins sucking on it. He cradles my thighs in his arms and just strings my orgasm out for what seems like forever. When I fall against the bed, limp and sweaty, he glances up at me with an expression of pure male pride on his face. "You are easy to please, female."

I gasp, and prop myself up on my elbows to look down at him. The hot alien just called me female instead of queen. He's accepting that there is some equality between us, and it's based on me being his woman. The feminist in me objects to being called female, like I'm just some nameless, faceless vagina. Unfortunately, the woman in me just body-slammed her and claimed victory.

"I'll give you that one, big guy. Now, get up here, and let's get to the good part." As I back up onto the bed, he moves in tandem with me with a sensual grace that I didn't know he had. The look on his face is fierce hunger. I reach out to stroke his cock and feel interesting ridges and rings under his flesh. I don't know for sure, but that feeds my kinky side. It's a side that I never knew I had until now.

He hisses with pleasure at my touch. When he awkwardly comes down on top me, I realize this must not be a preferred position for his kind. They're supposed to be submissive, so that makes sense. I spread my legs further apart and pull him gently down, positioning him where I want him to be.

His cock is already slick with pre-cum and he's actually dripping a bit. I love everything about this situation. I'm thrilled that he's a mess for me. It means he's excited and desperate to fuck from exploring by body and tasting me. His response to giving me oral sex is he's so excited that he's can barely hold back.

"Lay still, my female. I do not wish to injure you when I enter your body."

Running my hands over his muscular chest, I murmur, "Just go slow, and once I get used to you being inside me, you can move as fast as you want."

That statement earns me a sexy smile. He bullies himself in using a breathtaking series of short, sharp thrusts. Each one is measured and precise. Like most everything in his life, he does sex in a particular way, with utmost care and my safety in mind. The problem is, I don't want that. I want him wild with need and slightly out of control.

Allowing my hands to roam over his body, I look for more sensitive spots. I find one under his wing base, at the small of his back. When I touch him there, it causes him to thrust up sharply. His head snaps down to look into my eyes. His expression is hot but curious. When I use both hands to gently massage his wing base, he loses it a bit. Before long, he's thrusting into me hard and fast, and it feels absolutely amazing. I feel like I'm building to another amazing orgasm, but one of his hands drifts down, and his thumb hooks over my clit. By the time I figure out what he's doing, he's in control again.

Moments later, I'm locked down around him so tight that I don't think he could pull out if he wanted to. I'm coming so hard it feels like the top of my head is coming off. Suddenly, I'm being lifted from the bed. The moment my vaginal walls relax, Tabor is begins thrusting into me again. At some point, I realize that he's flapping his wings and this space has just enough room for him to lift me off the ground. The sensation of being fucked senseless by a hot warrior in mid-air after having two mind-blowing orgasms is nothing short of surreal.

His teeth clamp down on my neck where it meets the shoulder and his entire body convulses as he empties into me. It causes me to tip over into another orgasm as well. I didn't see that one coming. It kind of snuck up on me out of nowhere.

As his wings slow down and we float back down to the bed, I feel so profoundly connected to this man. This isn't just sex or joining, it's mating. No, the experience feels more like some primitive form of breeding. It's the combination of his unique musk, being so totally dominated and bitten as we both come again that makes it seem like more than just sex.

I'm glad he doesn't pull out when we hit the bed. Instead he rolls us until I am on top. Oh, he's good. Putting me on top is his smooth nonverbal way of putting me back in charge. I bring my hands up to cup his face, and we look into each other's eyes. "Hey there, handsome. If I get to decide when you pull out, it'll probably be never."

His hands come up to cover mine and he seems totally contented. "I would live the rest of my entire life nestled snugly in your beautiful cunt."

I'm shocked at his language again. "Babe, I know that word probably came up in your translation program, but we don't use it to refer to girl parts. You're going to have to pick another word from the selected list."

"I beg your pardon." I can tell that some small part of him enjoyed shocking me with a naughty word. It's cute, but if that word comes out of his mouth again, we're gonna rumble.

"You can always make up your own word for my girlie bits."

"We will call them queenly treasures because I do not approve of the term you use either. It implies I am touching a child."

Well, tonight is just turning out to be shock, shock, and more shock. This time there is no amusement in his voice, and it alerts me that my term is a hard no for him. "Queenly treasures it is, my love."

Her jerks slightly and pulls me face closer. "You have love for me?"

"I've never come right out and said it, but I love you very much."

"This is the strongest bond that humans are capable of forming, is it not?"

I nod slightly. It's hard because he's grasping my face pretty tight. It's not painfully tight but it does make moving problematic.

"This is also the way I feel about you. We do not have a word for the bond between a warrior and a queen for obvious reasons. Even a queen choosing a warrior as her Takadon did not come close to love as you know it. Takadon means he distinguished himself above her other breeders. The only word that resembles love as humans use the word is tankea. Tankea is the bond between a parent and child or between siblings and is considered sacred among our kind. I will now include you in the small group of people I tankea, my sweet female."

"You keep amazing me with the way you think, and how open you are about sharing yourself with me. When you talk to me about things like this, it helps me know you better, and that's the most important thing in my life right now."

"I value being close to you above all things now, as well, my tankea."

We snuggle up for hours, talking and making love all over again. Each time is better than the last. No one disturbs us for days. We order food from the dining hall, and it arrives by drone instead of by person. It takes me a minute to realize that it's because no one wants to smell Tabor's mating scent, nor do they want other women to be lured in by his scent. I laugh all the way through dinner over that.

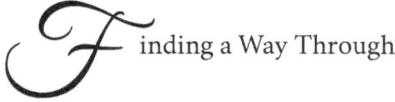inding a Way Through

~ Tabor ~

Kearney and I spend so many days that I lose count sequestered together in our quarters. We are making up for all the times when we were forced to forgo mating in favor of seeing to the needs of others. I do not know or much care what is going on outside our room. At some point the food becomes similar to what we ate on Earth. Sometime later we become aware that the ship is moving. My feeling of danger has been replaced with feelings of love and lust for my female. I have a female. To have been chosen and bred is the most fulfilling feeling a male can experience. To be selected by a soft human queen who allows a warrior to have his sexy way with her would have been impossible for me to imagine before experiencing it.

I now know why my brethren are so emotionally attached to their human mates. Human queens are as fascinated with us as we are with them. They attach to us and rely upon us for emotional support as well as protection.

Draconian queens use us for their pleasure and to breed, caring nothing for us as males. I've seen warriors so damaged after being bred by a Draconian queen that they required medical treatment. They use their claws and teeth on a male during mating and we never expect pleasure at their hands.

Even though I know it is the mind-controlling symbiont inside them that relishes inflicting pain, I much prefer my delicate soft human to the queens of old. She is all I need to find peace and happiness. I will show my gratitude to Elder Scarn and Darg for taking over my duties during my time of breeding.

I know that I am now with young. My side is swelling, my mating scent has faded, and my body temperature has shot up. Everything is as it should be. Even now my gentle queen is running her fingers over the slight bulge in my side. Two small bumps have risen. Since I was not bred to be a breeder, my offering of two will have to do. Before we can discuss what those bumps mean, we are interrupted by the ship shifting under our feet. I roll to my feet and grab my uniform. We are under attack. Though it will take much to penetrate our shields, I must make my way to the bridge. Kearney follows me to snatch on a clean uniform. "What do you think is going on?"

"I believe the Strovian is attacking us. We both know that he covets our queens."

"Their ship is huge. How are we going to stay out of their clutches."

We bolt down the corridor to the bridge. "Big ships are difficult to maneuver. I scanned his ship for weapons already and found we are equally matched."

When we rush onto the bridge, Scarn looks relieved but several other males twitch their noses. If I weren't focused on dealing with the interloper, I would be pleased to know they are offended by my now-fading mating scent.

"We are under attack by a Moltan vessel, commander. They have not made demands or asked us to surrender."

"I assume our shields are on maximum."

"Yes, commander, we've had them up since they first came into range and refused to identify themselves."

My queen slips into the seat beside me. "They're after our women. The Moltan were the ones experimenting with the symbionts. I think they may want test subjects. Since the symbionts only attach to females, we present a good target."

"Send out a general distress call. I want every ship in the area to know we are under attack by the Moltan."

"Already done, commander. That was one of the first things we did after raising the shields."

"The only ship to respond to our hail was Artor's, and he's on his way. We detected communication between Artor's vessel and the Moltan ship."

My queen sounds off her discontentment about that piece of information. "Why the hell are the Moltan talking to the Strovians but not us? That's kind of weird, considering they're attacking us and all."

I wrap my wing around her and give her my opinion. "One volley of cannon fire can hardly be called an attack. It was more like an attempt to engage us to give Artor time to join the fight. Together they could take us down and divide the queens."

"Then again they might screw up and blow us all up. They could also end up in a fight with each other after we're out of the game, where winner takes all. We need to get the hell out of this right now."

I rub my chin, considering our options. "I believe we should make an attempt to outrun the Moltan ship. If we can lose them, we will still have to face off with the Strovian vessel. However, we know how to best defeat Artor, and if we can claim a quick victory, then we can use his ship to fold space-time and easily get away from the Moltan vessel. We have successfully defeated the Moltan once before, but we have no time to fabricate liquid bombs and it is likely they will have evolved a strategy to counteract such measures."

"Agreed. Get us out of here, my takadon."

My new mate's trust in my judgement is humbling. I quickly look for options that might enable us to get away. "Are there any places for us to travel that would be difficult for the Moltan to track us?"

Drag's hands fly over his console, expertly adjusting his scanners. It takes a micron for him to look at his readings. In the meantime, the Moltan ship sends another lazy volley of shots towards our ship. "I may have something, commander. About three parsecs from our current location is a spectral event horizon. If we are careful and use filters on our external sensors, we might be able to navigate the anomaly and exit on the other side. I doubt any ship would follow."

Elder Scarn warns, "The Strovian vessel will know our strategy and simply fold space time and land on top of us."

My queen makes the final decision. "Do it, this is our best of some risky moves."

Darg reaches across his console and lays in a course for the event horizon. Pale gray filters drop into place over our sensors and we're suddenly in a world without color when looking outside the ship. It makes everything look dreary and strange to my eyes.

"I believe the Moltan vessel will throw everything they have at us once we begin moving away. They will want to keep us in place. Scarn, adjust our shields manually to concentrate our shielding to maximum capacity as we pass them and then put eighty percent of the shielding in the back. I don't want them getting through to our engines when firing from behind us."

"Yes, commander."

"What do you think our chances are, my takadon?"

"Every warrior here will fight to death to protect you and the other queens."

"That doesn't exactly answer my question, does it?"

"We will be victorious, because any other outcome is unacceptable."

"That's what I want to hear." She settles back against my side, and my chest aches at the thought of her losing her life because I could not protect her. Turning my attention back to the fight, our ship jolts over and over again as we move forward. We pick up speed and hit the event horizon at full force. Though our ship skids sideways, we remain intact and the Moltan ship remains in place outside the anomaly.

"I'm reorienting the ship to adjust for the push of the refracted light. Once I find the correct orientation, we should move through the anomaly more smoothly."

"You are doing a good job, Drag. Take your time. We gain nothing by rushing."

"Understood, commander." Some tension ebbs from his body as he works.

"Breaking free of the Moltan is but the first of many victories in this battle."

"I like where your head is, takadon."

I'm busy planning the next step in my strategy to defeat our enemies. "How long until we navigate through the anomaly?"

Drag whips his head around to reply. "At least three hours."

"I fear the Strovian ship will stop and allow the Moltan vessel to join in their energy field, enabling them both to transport to our location. Elder Scarn, I wish to devise the liquid bombs we used against the Moltan before. Though we may not have the same chemicals on board our vessel, I wish you to improvise."

"We have no way to transport the bombs aboard their vessels, commander."

"I am working on a plan for that as well. Please select warriors of worth, and work as quickly as possible. We will stay inside the anomaly until you have completed the incendiary devices. Remember to use the two-step process that was successful before. Perhaps if we are clever in our delivery, they might be caught unawares. If not, then we can at least stop the Strovian vessel with it."

My female's voice sounds off softly beside me, and I realize that I can think more clearly when she is near.

"You're really thinking of this from all angles, aren't you?" She's impressed by my intellect. Warriors are thought of as unintelligent and in need of queens to do their thinking. It angers me to find that much of what we have been taught is false.

"I was Meric's second for many years and have much experience in battle, my queen. I will not fail you."

"You don't need to waste a bunch of time reassuring me. I know you won't let me down."

"We need a clever ploy to get our incendiary devices aboard their ships without them realizing the danger. We will take out their weapons, then their engines."

"We could offer then the one thing they desire most."

"Never would I sacrifice a queen's life, even to save other queens."

"You wouldn't necessarily be sacrificing her, just putting her into an undesirable mating situation with the Strovians. Still, I was thinking something more along the lines of making a clone or creating an artificial bio sign that would trick their scanners into thinking a woman is in the pod."

I respond thoughtfully. "That's a good idea but there's no guarantee the weapons system will be close to their loading bay."

"If we figure that out, we could create a rocket that could penetrate their interior doors. We could aim it in the direction of their weapons and hope for the best."

An idea drops into my brain out of nowhere. "What if we used your idea of pods with human bio signatures, but hid tiny bots programmed to seek out and destroy their main power source?"

"I can think of about a hundred ways that could go wrong, but it's the best idea I've heard so far. I mean we've used bots on Earth for ages. We had ones to vacuum the floor before the turn of the century. Now they clean streets, windows, and even perform minor repairs. Phan injected tiny ones into your body to mend your artery back together. This might just be the answer we're looking for."

I can't be sure, but it appears that my mate just talked herself right into liking my idea. It's fascinating to see how her mind works. Human queens are extremely resourceful and adaptable.

My brother's voice came over the com. "We've been listening in on the mission planning and I've got an idea about how to get the bots out of the pod without anyone listening."

Pride surges though my chest that my Phan is contributing to our mission. "What is your idea, brother?" On most ships, acknowledging family ties would be considered unprofessional. Aboard a Draconian vessel, it is not, because we have so little family, acknowledging them is accepted practice.

"We could hide my medical bots in any viscous substance and have it rigged to leak if it is not handled with care. Chances are, once our enemy realizes our deception, they will abuse the pod. This is particularly true of Captain Artor. You said he appeared to have mood swings and difficulty controlling his anger and aggression. In any event, we can have them rigged to leak if they attempt to move it, or after a predetermined period of time. They will probably be quick to judge us as lacking in mechanical skills, since we're flying in such an old ship."

Queen Kearney asks, "Are you certain that you can program the bots to seek out their engines?"

"I can program them to do whatever we like. I would suggest that we program two sets of micro bots. One to seek out and destroy the engines and other set to seek out the air purification system and release a sedative."

I'm excited by my brother's suggestions. "Having a built-in redundancy plan is an excellent idea. It doubles our chances of success."

Phan's voice sounds pleased. "I'll begin programming the bots and human bio signatures immediately. Before you ask, I should have them finished within the next fifty microns."

Turning to my queen, I remark. "That is two and half hours in Earth time."

She elbows me gently in the side. "I know that, handsome. I've been hanging around your people for almost two years."

That we can find moments to jest even in such dangerous times gives me hope that we will continue to find true happiness together. In this moment, I know that I will do absolutely anything to protect her from the looming danger. No matter how complex this situation gets, I will find a way safely through it for my queen and the small roomful of child queens under my care.

cting Like an Alien

~ Kearney ~

We reassigned Elder Scarn from making incendiary devices to creating a viscous substance that would pass for lubrication. Not surprisingly, he chose actual lubricating fluid. We did darken the color to a deep blue to make it more difficult to see the micro bots. Of course we can't see them with the human eye, or a Draconian eye. However, they sometimes tend to clump together and can be noticeable if someone's paying close attention. Plus we don't know how good their vision is. They may be able to see things we can't, so it's best to do what we can to minimize the possibility of discovery.

I lean over the life pod that Scarn is working on. It's not really a life pod. It's something he threw together to look like one. "If you could back up, my queen, I would be able to concentrate better."

"I still smell like our commander's mating scent, don't I?"

"I would not wish to insult a queen, but the smell is repugnant."

I intentionally don't hit back on that only because we've got bigger fish to fry at the moment. "Do you think this will work?"

"With so many people contributing good ideas, I am very hopeful it will. If our efforts fail, and we are boarded, you are to take all the little ones and as many of the younger queens as possible into a shuttle and hide in the anomaly. We have sent a distress call, and that is where our people will look for us. We will keep them busy for as long as possible. Once you are out of harm's way, our strategy will no longer be victory. It will be stringing out the battle for as long as possible with the goal of keeping our enemies off you while waiting for our brethren to join the fight."

"Why didn't Tabor tell me this?"

"Because he will wish to delay telling you for as long as possible in case we are forced to stun you to ensure you get on the shuttle."

"I won't leave. This is my ship and I'll die fighting."

"We cannot mount an effective battle strategy if we have queens to protect. Would you risk Tabor's life only for the privilege of staying at his side? You are no warrior, Queen Kearney. The younger queens need someone who can think fast and solve complex problems. You have a duty to them, just as we have a duty to you. Do not shame your takadon by refusing to allow him to fight for you."

I feel a sharp pain lancing through my chest. My God, he's right. We've all got our part to play in this and I cannot escape mine any more than Tabor can escape his. "I've always felt in control of my destiny. Now, I feel as though my life is already set in motion with me only needing to step through the motions of living it."

"It is times like these that test the limits of our sanity and make us weary of the bonds we have made with others. I have lost much in my life. I was once a breeder to a ruthless Draconian queen and none of my young pleased her. Being forced to stand by and watch all of my babies be reaped, one at a time, broke my spirit. I never thought to care for another being in my lifetime. Signing onto this ship has been my salvation, for not only did I form close friendships with Tabor, Phan, and Timric, but I also discovered that not all queens are evil. Sleeping with a kind queen in my arms has restored my faith in the 'verse. Entares may have turned her back on me in my youth, but the goddess doubled back to smile on an elder warrior who thought his time was coming to an end. Trust in the goddess, and never lose hope, Queen Kearney."

"I can understand why Draconians believe elders are full of wisdom. If the worst comes to pass, I will put duty first."

"I'm afraid you can do nothing else when tiny humans are relying upon you for their safety."

He stops, wipes his hands, and adds a small, thin sheet of metal around the interior of the pod. "This is specially coated metal that will keep the enemy from locking onto the bio-signal securely. They will likely think their sensors are picking up a female in stasis."

"Draconians are clever, and you think of everything."

"Thank you, Queen Kearney. Will you check that your mother and the other queens are well?'

"I can see you're really trying to get rid of the mating scent. I'll jump in the mister if it's that distracting."

"Though the odor is not as potent, it's difficult to express how unpleasant it is. I would rather smell ten-day-old garbage than our commander's scent."

"I've heard breeders stink up the entire ship. I guess my mom's going to be taking a lot of showers to get your mating scent off her."

Elder Scarn actually drops the tool he's working with. "Your mother wishes me for a mate? She calls me her bed warmer. I thought all human females had them."

"That's not remotely true. We bring males into our bed that we want to have romantic relations with."

"Romantic relations means mating, am I right?"

"I'm afraid so. Don't worry. My mother would die a thousand

cruel deaths before allowing anything to happen to your hatchlings."

His eyes take on a faraway look, and he seems to be lost in his own thought for a few moments. He snaps out of it, commenting wishfully, "She does love small humans. Perhaps she will grow a likening for our young as well."

"Don't be a knucklehead. Any children she has with you will mean the world to her."

Scarn does not seem to know how to process this information. Maybe I messed up by being so open about my mother's affection for him. I should mention that I messed up there to her, so she's not blindsided by it.

I head for her quarters, feeling a bit useless. All the warriors are busy executing our plan, and I'm wandering around bothering them. That's not okay, since I'm a grown woman, and not an attention-seeking child."

Along the way I bump into one of the Grayson clan, and she's furious. Shoving another girl down, she screams. "You will obey my every word if you wish to live. I have no tolerance for other queens in my private space."

"Hold up, what's going on here?"

"I do not answer to you or any other human queen."

I take a minute to look her up and down. "Why the hell are you talking like an alien? I don't know what kind of game you're playing, but you sound all kinds of crazy, so you might want to button it up."

An enraged look crosses her face, and she lunges for me. She's all fancy gown and flying hair, and she's pissing me off. Just before she makes contact, I kick my foot right into her chest, and it sends her sprawling back onto her ass. I walk over, and squat down in front of her. "You and I are both human, dumbass. We're out in the black of space with enemies trying to kill us. If you don't let go of the crazy and calm your ass down, I'm gonna lock you in your room. Am I making myself clear?"

She leans forward and inhales. "You are the ranking breeding female on this ship. That fact alone makes you my enemy."

"Okay, I've had enough." Grabbing her by the arm, I haul her up to her feet, put my hand on the back of her neck and perp-walk her squawking ass to her room. Ordering the other woman out, I fling her inside and use my hand to bio-lock the door. Turning to the two shocked women, I ask, "What the hell was that all about?"

I don't recognize these members of Grayson's clan. The one with red hair shakes her head but doesn't speak. Her long curls are cute as hell, but she's not coming through with the information I want. The brunette gestures towards the door. "She was fine before she came aboard your ship. Since she arrived, she's been getting bitchier and more condescending. It kind of comes and goes, but it's been increasing in intensity. We've been trying to steer clear of her, but she's seems to always be spoiling for a fight."

"Maybe her life isn't turning out quite how she intended. Her quaint little imitation of aliens isn't going to help her fit in around these parts."

"Do you think she has some kind of space dementia?"

I snort a laugh. "No, I think she's young, anxious, and attention-seeking."

"Are you letting her out of the room?"

"Hell no, she's lucky I don't toss her in the brig. I don't know if you two know it or not, but we're in a fight for our lives against two superior opponents. If we don't end up getting distracted by foolishness like this, we just might survive and make it to our new home world. I'm locking her down until we're out of the danger zone. Chilling in her room for a few days won't kill her. She's got a private bath, and I want you two to see she gets fed. All the doors have a slot for drone delivery, so don't ask for a door override."

"We aren't looking for any trouble. Where are we supposed to stay?"

"Neither of you are in trouble. I just want you to understand our situation so you can make good decisions for yourself. I'm on my way to my mother's suite. If you come along, I'll get her to sort you out with another room temporarily." When they don't answer, I turn on my heel and walk off, barely aware that they're following me.

My mother has just put the twins down for a nap when we arrive. She places a finger to her mouth, a gesture for us to be quiet. After she closes the door to their room, we are free to talk.

She tip-toes across the room before speaking quietly. "How's the battle going, Keary?"

"We've got plans nestled inside of plans. I'd be surprised if our warriors lost this battle. Unfortunately, unexpected things are always happening so it's difficult to say for sure. Speaking of unexpected things happening, I ran into one of Virgil's kin acting all kinds of crazy. She tried to attack me, and I had to lock her in her room. If you can possibly believe it, she was talking like an alien. She called me a human queen and said since I was the breeding queen in charge I was her enemy."

My mother wrinkled her nose in distaste. "That is strange. I wonder what that's all about?"

The redhead finally speaks up. "Samantha's not herself. She's normally really cooperative."

My mother turns curious eyes on me. "There must be some explanation for why she's acting so weird. Any idea at all what could be driving this change in behavior, Keary?"

"Hell if I know, but we can't allow her to go running around picking fights with the other women, which leads me to our next problem. Her two roommates need a place to stay."

"I think that's something can be worked out. Would you all like to stay and chat while I look at my list? I made some coffee."

"I hate to call my own mother a liar, but we don't have coffee on this ship."

"That's where you're wrong. Scarn spent a small fortune on coffee beans. He's as addicted to it as I am. After doing without for so long, nothing tastes better than a nice cup of java."

"I see how it is. You're getting spoiled, and I'm getting to choose between which of our enemies to kill first. That hardly seems fair." My voice is light to disguise my anxiety about speaking the truth.

My mother's head jerks up, "Kearney Sue, tell me you aren't trying to kill people."

I cringe at her tone. "No, we're just trying to disable their ships so they don't destroy our vessel. There's no denying that if it comes down to it we might have to crack a few skulls."

Her disapproval bothers me. "I don't like the flippant way you talk about death."

"Me either, but you have to understand that Kendra and I have been surviving out in the black for a while now. We have to do what's necessary to survive. I can't say we've ever killed anyone ourselves, but the warriors protecting us have. I know it's hard to get your head around but if our choices are to stay on Earth and slowly waste away or take to space and fight, the latter at least ensures our survival."

Her expression shifts from disapproving to frustrated. "I just can't believe it's come down to this."

"Unfortunately, human women are coveted in this sector of space. That means some people break the law in order to get ahold of us. I don't want any of us ending up in some alien brothel or on an alien's plate for dinner. We have the right to protect ourselves. It would be nice if you could get on board with that."

"I have to admit that if it came down to it I'd kill to protect my children or the other women here. I suppose that I'm not all that different from you. I've just been struggling in a different kind of way for survival on Earth."

I wrap my arms around my mother, feeling horrible for being so hard on her. "I'm sorry, mom. I just need us all to be on the same page. There's strength in numbers."

"I'll do whatever's necessary."

Holding her back at arm's length, I see the last couple of years haven't been kind. She's aged at least eight or ten years since I last saw her. "Scarn talked about what to do if we're boarded, right?"

She nods, her face a mask of pain. "I hate the warriors staying behind to fight, but we have the little ones to protect."

"That's literally the only thing that could pull me away from Tabor. Let's hope it doesn't come down to that."

"I'll pray it doesn't, cause I don't think we'd be very good at standing between danger and the children if all the warriors get taken out."

"We're pretty smart and resourceful, so I honestly don't think that will happen."

Just then my com goes off. "Queen Kearney, we need you in the medical unit immediately."

My mother tosses me a weak smile. "Women's work is never done, in space as well as on Earth."

"Don't worry, I'll keep you posted."

ealing in Deceit

~ Tabor ~

I hover over my brother and his mate as they work on the bots. She's taking each one out and fitting it into a tray with small magnetic pinchers. She looks so much like my sweet queen that my heart aches to see her. She's currently wearing a visor that magnifies the bots so she can see them. When she glances up at me, her blue eyes look huge and comical. She goes back to work, and I have to admire her diligence. Her motions are smooth and quick.

Though she's impressive, I prefer watching my brother. He puts the trays in a specially designed machine and then keys in the commands for each bot. My brother may not be the biggest or the strongest warrior, but he is one of the smartest. He's half healer and half scientist but all warrior. It is a combination which earns him honor and respect among our people. My father and I worked hard to keep him pointed in the right direction and focused on his studies and now that effort has paid off. I have no words to describe how proud I am of him for his part in saving our queens this day.

They are nearly finished, and Elder Scarn is pacing back and forth in the loading bay waiting to load the bots and bio-signature devices into the pods. Once that is done, all we have to do is wait for our enemies to arrive. There can be no doubt they heard us issue a distress call, therefore they will wish to flush us out as soon as possible.

My queen slips in the door unnoticed by all but me. "Are you well, my queen?" I don't know why I'm asking, but I scented danger on her when she came close.

"I'm fine. There was a problem with one of the women acting out, but I handled it."

"We are finishing up the bots. Phan has already programed the bio signatures and they have been locked into place in the pods."

"Elder Scarn explained plan B to me in terms I could understand. The only reason I agreed to abandon you to the fight is because he said I'm no good at fighting and you would be distracted protecting me instead of fighting."

Anger flared hot in my chest. "He had no right to tell you that. When this is all over, I will have words with him over this."

She steps forward and wraps her arms around my waist. "Don't bother. I needed to hear it from an elder. I never would have listened to you."

"I don't know whether to be pleased at your dedication or upset that you would not obey your protector when danger is near."

"You can be both."

I wrap her up in my arms, praying to the goddess that our plan works. By plan, I do not mean the one involving bots. I have already run the stats on that plan, and there is only a forty-two percent chance it will be effective. I mean our plan to cover the escape of our queens in the two shuttles.

Every warrior on this ship is fairly certain that this is not a battle we will survive. Elder Scarn and I have decided that our youngest two recruits will pilot the two shuttles. They are scarcely of age and none of us can bear the thought of losing them. I have yet to break the news to them. Denying the young warriors the opportunity to fight and die for their queens will make them furious. They will have to deal with their emotions because none of the queens can fly a shuttle. Plus, I hate to say it, but they will be the last line of resistance if the shuttles are boarded.

None of us have the heart to speak of this to the queens or young warriors. Though I wish Elder Scarn had let me speak to my queen in the due course of time, part of me is grateful for being spared the agony of that conversation. I hold her tighter, as the feeling of danger grows ever stronger. I would curse my gift of knowing, if it did not give a slight advantage in protecting my love.

Nothing about this day except having my lovely queen in my arms pleases me. When my brother is finished, he has ten thousand bots encased in two tiny metal boxes, one for each pod. That they are all piled on top of each other is the only way I know they are there. These are somewhat larger than the ones he injected into my bloodstream, but not by much. We head down to the loading bay, and I can hear messages broadcasting over our com. They are dark and foreboding messages of doom and destruction as our enemies try to force us from our hiding place. We pay them no mind and continue with our plan.

Darg's voice comes over the com. "Commander, the Strovian vessel did not stop for the Moltan ship to join forces. They are boxing us in, and each firing into the event horizon."

"It is as I expected them to do. I will come to the bridge and speak with them, after we load the bots into the pods." I don't know why it is important, but I think overseeing this process is important. Maybe I'm just stalling for time. My own motivation is lost to me at this point.

Elder Scarn turns as we enter and rushes over to the first pod. He's set up two vats of lubricant. Phan empties one box of bots into each vat. We watch them clump together even though Scarn stirs the viscous liquid. "Can we add something with a higher viscosity to thin the mixture?"

My Kearney agrees. "If we could thin it down a little, maybe they wouldn't clump together so much."

Elder Scarn opens a small metal jug and pours a dribble of liquid into each vat. When he stirs them again, the bots are much less noticeable. "That's much better."

He closes each vat and attaches it to the underside of the pod. His engineering is excellent. The bot housing units have metal tubes attached and appear to be part of the initial design of the pod.

"That's the best I can do." The older man sounds satisfied with his work, but it remains to be seen how effective our ruse will be. We head to the bridge. Instead of upbeat, we are solemn and anxious.

I speak with the Moltan first, even though I know they will not answer. "Stand down your attack and we will send you a human female. We do not wish to part with our females, but we will sacrifice one for the safety of all." They stop firing at us. Even though their shots were not landing on our vessel with all the refracting going on inside the event horizon, it's progress in the right direction.

I shift my attention to Artor on the Strovian ship. "Stand down you attack, Artor. We are prepared to give you one human female if you stop your attack on our vessel."

His face appears almost instantaneously on our screen. "I wish to choose the female from your collection myself."

"No. You get the one we select."

A stubborn look crosses his face. "You have my chosen mate, and I want her delivered to me immediately."

My queen steps forward to speak with the ignorant man herself. "What are you talking about?"

"I wish to have the queen who sat beside me while we dined on your distasteful human food. She has hair the color of fire."

She whispers, "He's talking about Crazy Pants. She attacked me today, and I had to put her on lock down. She was talking like an alien, calling me human, and saying I was her enemy."

I turn to the view screen and lie. "We know of the female you speak of. She attacked my mate. We are happy to be rid of her. Do you agree to cease hostilities if we deliver her to you unharmed?"

"We accept your offer, but be warned. My bride had better not have one scratch on her pale body."

"We have made the same deal with the Moltan. We will deliver both your brides momentarily."

The screen goes blank, and I message Elder Scarn. "Are you ready to launch the pods?"

Since pods are designed to shoot off from a ship under fire like a rocket in order to avoid being taken out by an explosion, I designed these pods in the same manner. "They should only take about three or four microns to exit the event horizon on either side."

"Thank you for all your hard work on the pods, Elder Scarn. I guess, we will know when they take the pods aboard if our ruse works."

"It is my best work, Queen Kearney." The elder's voice is thick with emotion, for he is not used to being praised so openly by a queen.

My queen's bottom lip quivers but she forces herself to speak. "I want you to know that no matter how this day ends, I've been proud to have you as a father for the last few weeks. My mother chose well when she selected you as her bed warmer."

"I live to serve, both my queen and her daughters. If thing go badly, live the life we would have wished for you, my daughter."

I pull my queen close under my wing, as she fights back tears. "Eject the pods at your discretion, Elder Scarn."

We hear silence, then the clicking of machinery. The elder's voice chokes out, "Pods away, commander."

We wait with anxiety twisting in our stomachs, and I feel it the moment things go wrong. The Moltan lock onto their pod with a tractor beam and know immediately that they have been tricked. Instead of pulling it into their ship, they fire on it, and we watch it explode along with any hopes of avoiding an all-out battle. "Move closer to the Strovian vessel. Get us as far away from the Moltan as possible without leaving the shelter of the anomaly." The Moltan begin firing into the event horizon and it takes the Strovians only a moment later to open their pod. Then they are incensed as well. "Artor seems reluctant to fire upon our ship."

"Maybe he doesn't want to risk killing his bride. I'd give my first born to know why he's so obsessed with her and why she's acting so weird."

"Don't give away our first born just yet, my queen."

Drag states excitedly from his station. "The Strovian ship has launched a fighter, commander."

"Elder Scarn, activate our back up plan. Phan and Timric report to Elder Scarn for orders. You are being assigned a special mission, one of the utmost importance. You will follow his orders without hesitation. The lives of almost two hundred queens depend upon your bravery today."

Both warriors acknowledge the command. I release my queen very reluctantly and we stand, facing each other. With the battle erupting around us, there isn't enough time or privacy for the kind of farewell I wish to make with her. Because she is my mate, she senses my dilemma.

Cupping my face in her hands, her eyes fill with tears. "On ancient Earth women told their mates to come home victorious or on their shield."

I know that 'on their shield' means dead because I am a warrior. I struggle to find words to convey what is in my mind and in my heart.

Running her thumbs across my jawline like she is wont to do, she looks into my eyes. Her bottom lip quivers again. It breaks my heart to see her like this.

"I'm not from ancient Earth, so I'm just going to demand that you fight with your sharp mind and your skills as a warrior. You are it for me, my takadon. If you do not live, I will not take another mate. I will dedicate myself to the little ones and live for the day we meet again in the hereafter."

"I will do my best to survive and be victorious."

"No matter how the battle goes, if you do your best, I will live with the outcome."

I dip my head and take a kiss that is so much less than I need to sustain me through this battle. "Go my love, do not keep the others waiting."

"Fight well, my takadon, and know you are in my heart." She turns quickly, and it's as if she has to force her feet to move. When they do, she breaks out into a run.

I find my eyes are leaking water like a human. Our kind does not cry, yet I do. I feel more emotion than ever before, so maybe I've just never allowed myself to feel enough to cry. When I return to my seat, the other males are shocked. I can see it on their faces. I wipe at my face and steel myself for the fight to come.

"Once the shuttles launch, we will destroy the fighter the Strovians launched and then circle back around to the Moltan. Our fight is with them since the Strovians either will not or cannot fire on us again. Although the bots might have been more successful than we ever imagined, I also believe they fired on us before at less than full force, hoping to frighten us. Well, I am not frightened, and we will renew our fight with them after vanquishing the Moltan. We will give the bots a chance to work their magic upon Captain Artor and his crew."

 aught in The Middle

~ Kearney ~

The fight is not going well. We are caught between two enemies and both are stronger and more well-armed. Virgil and his sons are staying to fight. I'm not surprised, cause he loves to mix it up with anyone he can. I stoop to pick up a little girl crying in the loading bay and we begin to fill the two shuttles. Scarn has had to take out all the seats and there is literally standing room only. My knees grow weak when I realize we don't have room for all the women.

The elders are sorting them by age, with the oldest electing to stay behind. I know why they're doing this, but it feels so wrong. We all had to take the lifeboat test in school, where you had to decide which people to save in an end-of-the-world situation. I struggled really hard with the test, going back and forth until I ran out of time. They do it so effortlessly that it pains my soul.

My mother is standing firm by Scarn's side, and it takes me a minute to realize she's staying behind. I have a moment of not being able to cope. Everything's moving too fast, and I didn't come all this way to save everyone in my family but her. Her eyes tell me what her mouth can't, and Phan pulls me into the shuttle he has been tasked with piloting. Kendra is at his side and appears to be learning to drive the shuttle from watching his movements.

Grayson and his sons are saying their own goodbyes to their womenfolk, and it helps me see the gruff men in a whole new light. Virgil jerks his chin in acknowledgement of seeing me. I suck it up and yell out to him. "If we make it out of this alive, we're each gonna have a ship armed to the teeth and create our own little armada."

He grins and shoves Donna into our shuttle. The poor woman is in tears. I wrap my arm around her, wondering how she got a spot, but my mother didn't. They're roughly the same age. It hits me hard and fast that my mother chose to stay to enable younger or simply other women to go. When they close the door, I feel the chill all the way down to my bones. Swallowing thickly, I turn to Phan. "Get us the hell outta here, Phan. I want you to maneuver out to the edges as far from the enemy ships as possible. Especially stay away from the Moltan, cause they're slap happy today."

"It will be as you wish, Queen Kearney." He deftly maneuvers the controls with both hands, his brow creased with concentration.

I turn and give the little one to one of the other women. The little one is rubbing her eyes and crying. I hate that everyone is so upset, but I can see that the little ones are getting consoled. Moving up to the navigation console gets me a better view of the raging battle.

They've put the grey visors over our sensors, so we aren't blinded by all the refraction of light. Some of it is denser than others, so we ride it like waves. Phan and Timric communicate with each other, and the shuttles dance around each other like a choreographed routine. When I see it, I think they must have chosen them to pilot our shuttles because they are battle buddies, and attuned to each other's flying and fighting style. The shuttles now have gigantic laser rifles mounted to the four corners. That must have been compliments of Scarn and his team, when they were waiting for Phan to finish programing the bots. The Moltan ship is firing at my vessel, but my crew is skillfully maneuvering around, missing most of the shots, without returning fire. I'm impressed with the old ship's maneuverability.

Phan mumbles, "My brother is spending down the fuel rods on their energy weapons. It's a good strategy."

Since I have no idea how much energy those massive laser cannons burn through with each burst, I can't get my head around how effective that tactic will be. I do trust my takadon though. If it's possible for this battle to end with none of our crew being killed, Tabor will see it done. I know that's a pretty tall order, but my commander is clever and resourceful.

Suddenly, the sky lights up the Moltan vessel. I reach for the grab bar over Phan's head and lean in to get a better look.

Kendra grabs onto my arm. "What's going on? Are there more people joining the fight?"

Phan answers before I can. "We're getting incoming messages from the Raspian. They're responding to our distress call. They can't fit inside the anomaly but our crew is joining them against the Moltan."

Sure enough, our ship had slipped out of the event horizon on the side with the Moltan vessel, and both ships had lit up the space around the Moltan like the fourth of July. We watch the enemy ship detonate and the shielded escape pod explode while in the process of breaking off. I know immediately that they just didn't launch in time to clear the explosion. Knowing living beings have been killed sends a chill up my spine. Yet, the battle is only half over.

I place my hand on Phan's shoulder. "Take us to the Raspian. I want to unload the women and come back to help Tabor fight off the Darnovo."

"That is the Strovian vessel?"

"Yes. He's not emitting his identification beacon, but that's the name of his ship." He hastily turns the shuttle around and makes for the Raspian. "It's no longer moving but the engines are still online."

"Since the weapons are still offline, I'm hopeful it can be boarded without incident."

Phan speaks without looking up from his navigational array. "If we can secure the Darnovo ship it will be a good addition to your trade armada."

I forage through my memories until I remember the rules regarding space battles. "I forgot the intergalactic laws regulating this sector of space for a moment. When ships do battle, the winner takes all."

"Yes, my queen. That is the law."

"Well, it would have suited me just fine if he'd left when he had the chance. Truth be told, I think Captain Artor would be better off without a ship. Being mobile just seems to get him into trouble wherever he goes."

As we move closer to the Raspian, we see dozens of small fighters swarming from their launch bay. They head straight for the event horizon and buzz right past our shuttle. "I get the strong feeling this battle is going to be over before we can unload the women and get back through the anomaly."

My sister answers quietly, "From your lips to God's ear."

ictory

~ Tabor ~

As luck would have it, the Raspian was not too far from our current location. They destroyed the Moltan vessel and sent fighters to assist me with the Darnovo. We're in our loading bay, gearing up to board the Darnovo. The ship's weapons are down, and it's drifting, dead in space. Still, boarding her will be an entirely different story. The Strovians will be armed to the teeth, and raring to fight the battle they were denied in space.

I've left a skeleton crew on the bridge, and every warrior we can spare is preparing to board the enemy ship. Even the humans are happily gearing up for the fight. Unlike their females, they seem to relish hand-to-hand combat.

Their eyes light up as my crew members teach them how to attach body armor. Laser rifles are similar in operation to the rifles they brought with them. It doesn't take long for them to see the advantage of a weapon you don't have to reload. We can get around a hundred shots out of laser weapon before needing to slam another battery pack into place. We each ring our belts with extra battery packs amongst the knives and laser pistols.

The plan is for us to attach our ship to the Darnovo's docking ring, infiltrate the ship and open the loading-bay doors for the fighters. Then we will sweep the ship, break through any resistance, and take as many prisoners as possible. Even though the Intergalactic Council can't interfere in the internal disputes with member worlds, they can and do have lawmen and courts to prosecute intergalactic criminals that prey on member worlds.

The moment we attach and the docking ring opens, we step through. In the loading bay we see the fake life pod they pulled in and several Strovian bodies lying about. My brother's bots had rendered them unconscious. We secured them and began working our way across the ship to the loading bay. The docking bay is typically on the opposite side as the loading bay, one being for visitors, and the other for freight.

Virgil is on one side and Elder Scarn the other. The human tugs on the neck of his armored uniform. "This is a huge damn ship. Are you sure you know where we're going, commander?"

I know the human is just making conversation to take the edge off. They aren't career soldiers, nor have they been trained as warriors.

"Step lightly and keep your eyes and ears open."

He replies dryly, "Ya, they have the home court advantage."

Unsure what that means, I just nod and lead the way. We encounter resistance, and the situation quickly devolves into a shooting match. Their red laser fire is met by our blue fire. Their light blue armor looks childish compared to dark Draconian battle armor. It's not as effective either. Our weapons tear through their armor with very little effort.

Scarn catches my eye. His face looks strange with the bubble shield all around. It is a relatively new invention for our people, and I'm not sure I like it. "Something is wrong. This is too easy."

"We fight, they lose. It is the will of the goddess." I think it's too easy as well, but I have no more explanation than Scarn. I can feel something huge, dark and menacing. My senses tell me it's mechanical and very near. There are three triple doors leading from the rest of the ship to the cargo bay and one gigantic bay door opening on the far side leading to space. The bay is dark with red blinking lights running around the middle of the way. There isn't a person in sight.

Scarn moves close to me as we step thorough one of the doors. We make our way towards the gigantic bay door to the center console. There is shielding between us and the bay door. Once the fighters land, we'll close the doors, depressurize the bay, and lower the shields. Our forty warriors will turn into nearly seventy, which will be enough to take the rest of the ship. It's a good plan.

Virgil screams over the com. "Look to the ceilings."

Our laser rifles all jerk up, and that's when we see them. Huge mechanical robots begin unfolding from the ceiling. It makes sense. Where we have been focusing on improving our armor and skills, they have been working on building a better soldier. We light the room up with laser fire and the humans go a little wild. Nothing we shoot at them seems to slow them down.

I see one of Virgil's sons climbing up a bot, while the rest of his family keeps it busy. He blasts open the back of the bot's helmet and tosses in a plasma grenade. That seems to be the magical combination. I begin shouting orders to my crew, as more of the bots drop. The bots are five times our size and have revolving lasers around each wrist. I can practically see my personal shield being drained before my very eyes. We all step our game up and work in small groups to take down each bot.

At some point I realize that they have more than we can successfully defeat. As my crew continues the battle, I try to discover where they're coming from. That's when I see the feeding lines running across the ceiling, pulling in more and more of them, dropping them into the fray. I shoulder my laser rifle, flap my wings, and take flight in the gigantic bay. I know that I'm taking a chance of my wings getting damaged with all the laser fire flying around, but we need a miracle right now, and this might be it.

The bots must have sensors because the moment I get close they begin grabbing for me. I artfully dodge their grasp. After searching for what seems like forever as the battle rages on below me, I finally see what appears to be a gearbox and take aim. A huge metal hand closes around my arm. Another grabs my leg, and I realize they are attempting to immobilize me. My one chance is to make the gear box inoperable. Another bot's gigantic hand closes around my wing base. Though my personal shield is still operable, the pressure is causing it short out. With my one free hand, I grab for the laser pistol on my hip. I aim and fire, leaving a gaping hole. I drop the pistol, snag a plasma grenade, and toss it into the hole.

One micron later, the box explodes, peppering my energy shield with shards of metal. The cables stop pulling more drones out, and I'm left trying to free myself from the bots, which are still very active. Suddenly, Virgil leaps off the catwalk and land on the bot's back. He blows open the back of its skull casing and drops in a plasma grenade. When the bot lets go I'm at an awkward position. If not for my wings, I would have fallen onto the metal floor below with only my now-failing shield to break my fall.

Once I touch down on the floor, my crew is taking down the last of the bots. I rush over and open the gigantic bay doors and the fighters swarm in, landing in neat little rows. Each fighter holds one warrior, so many can fit on the cleared side of the bay.

Once we are all ready, we begin clearing the rest of the Strovians out of the ship. There are fewer of them than I would have thought. I suppose that is because this is a rebel ship, and they rely upon the bots to do most of their fighting.

We make it to the bridge, and I'm finally face-to-face with Captain Artor. "Where is my bride, Dracon?" His smooth blue skin is blotched with purple marks. And he seems off balance. The rage I expected is nowhere to be found. His only interest is the female.

Lowering my rifle slightly, I stare at him. "You have no female, Artor. No human queen has chosen you."

He's sweating, and I notice his hair is stringy. "We shared the bonding elixir. I put some in her drink and in my own. If she but sees me, she will claim me." He cranes his head and trembles slightly. Anyone could tell he's ill.

"I will have my bride." He roars so loudly he almost topples over. If he weren't holding onto a console with one hand, he would have fallen. I jerk my chin to Scarn, and my longtime friend lifts his laser rifle. His finger flips it to stun and he shoots. They put the confused villain in stasis and cart him off to his own medical bay. His remaining crew members are taken to the brig. I breathe a sigh of relief that this is over, but the uneasy feeling in my stomach will not go away.

I reach to my ear and open a private line to Phan.

He answers immediately. "Yes, commander."

"I need a medic."

"I'm dropping off the women aboard our ship now. We were going to take them to the Raspian, but they are leaving on a clandestine mission and cannot risk having extra queens on board."

"Drop them off at our ship and bring the female that Queen Kearney locked away for her own safety. Captain Artor is sick. We will use the medical bay aboard the Darnovo to examine them."

My queen's voice sounds in my ear. "I'm coming as well."

"All will be as you wish, my queen. I will meet you at docking ring nine myself."

"Are you well, my takadon?" I can hear her concern for me in the tone of her voice.

"I am well, and the Darnovo has been secured, my queen."

"Good, because I've decided that I'm trading up."

"You have chosen wisely, my queen. I must point out that we will not be permitted to keep the device that folds space time."

"I rather thought that might be too good to be true."

"It is considered proprietary alien technology. We do not know how to use such advanced equipment, in any event. It can be dangerous in the wrong hands."

"Send word to the Strovians that they need to come and remove it from my new ship. Let them know that we are turning the rebels over to the Intergalactic Council." My queen didn't sound all that disappointed to be losing out on such coveted tech.

"Yes, my queen. I look forward to seeing you shortly."

We turn our attention to familiarizing ourselves with basic Strovian technology. Ships' systems all have some similarities, and Draconian warriors are good at figuring out puzzles. We trace the relays, used our translation programs to help us access the ship's database and slowly transition full control of the ship over to our control. Carefully locking out all the Strovian frequencies was tedious, but necessary so they couldn't take control of the ship back.

vil Scientist

~ Kearney ~

Standing in the medical bay aboard the Darnovo, we watch Phan run scans of both Captain Artor and the woman from the Grayson clan he's identified as his intended bride. Phan has a human woman I recognize working at his side. I rush over to the console she's using to run diagnostic. "Stacy, it's nice to have another doctor on board."

She glances up with a welcoming smile. "I was on the Raspian with Meric and after hearing the symptomology I had to come and have a look for myself." She's wearing a set of white scrubs. Alien scrubs are styled after uniforms, only white with green piping.

"Do you think she's contracted something nasty on Earth that's been slowly making her sick?" I only ask that because I'm fairly certain it's the only explanation that makes sense.

"I don't want to alarm you, but the initial readings suggest she might be infected by a Draconian queen symbiont."

A chill creeps up my spine. "That's not possible. We killed the queen and burned her ash on the metal floor."

"I remember when Meric, Tabor, and our crew ended her life. Even though it might not seem possible, the woman is infected."

"How?"

"Not many know, but the Moltan vented a sample from the queen's body into space."

I stand gaping at her. What kind of sample? How large was it?

Phan looked up from his scanner. "The Strovian captain is infected as well."

We both gasp at the same time. Stacy steps over to look at the scanner. "It looks like the symbiont is attacking his organs rather than trying to gain a foothold in his body like it does with women."

Phan frowns. "I might need the female DNA marker to propagate." Suddenly, he freezes and Stacy's mouth drops open.

"You might have just discovered the key to ensuring no one else ever becomes infected by the symbionts." Stacy begins scrolling through his information. "It's possible we can program micro bots to clear out the symbiont."

The two healers begin to brainstorm ways to eliminate the symbiont, and I take a moment to slip over and have a quiet work with my takadon. "You're looking a little rough around the edges, handsome. Are you sure you're okay?"

Opening his arms, he draws me close. "My body armor and shield held up. The odds were not in our favor, but the goddess smiled on us today."

"Humans have a saying for situations like that. We call it pulling victory from the jaws of defeat."

His eyes turn warm, and his hands begin to move over my arms. "It is a good saying."

"I'm really proud of our crew, and you most of all. You worked together and saved a lot of women today."

"We live to serve, my gracious queen. Did I understand you to say you were intent upon claiming the Darnovo as a battle prize?"

"Why not? It's well within my rights."

"What does one small queen need with two ships?"

"Being out in the black has taught me the 'verse is a very unpredictable place. I believe a small armada would make transporting goods safer. We'll move onto the Darnovo and the Graysons can borrow our ship until they earn enough to buy their own vessel. We'll make runs side by side."

"This ship is huge, modern and well-maintained. It's also populated with large robots that can be repurposed to handle cargo. Making this the flagship of your armada is a wise decision, my ambitious queen."

Jumping up onto my toes, I give him a kiss on his chin. "Yep, I'm smart that way."

Before he can reply, the door slides open. Scarn and my mother walk in. She walks over to me, and we hug briefly. Before I ask how she's doing, she begins speaking. "I heard about the Strovian Captain being sick, and I've been thinking that it's pretty much of a coincidence that he's sick and the woman he's obsessed with is sick as well. I began talking to all the womenfolk in the Grayson clan. One of them saw the Strovian put something into her drink at the restaurant."

My anger flares hot as a supernova. "Why in the hell didn't she say something before now?"

My mother's lips firm into a thin line. "She thought it was some kind of alcohol or drink enhancer. She said he looked respectable, he smiled at her, and she caught his eye."

Stacy spoke up from near the scanner. "That sounds like the point of origin for the illness."

Tabor frowns, "Captain Artor said something about putting the elixir of life in their drinks. He said it was supposed to make her chose him for her mate. He said all she has to do is see him."

Stacy rubs her temple with one hand. I'm beginning to get a migraine from the stress of this situation as well, so I understand how she feels. "It sounds like someone has been filling his head full of nonsense. They probably figured out what he wanted most, and then sold the elixir to him as the way of obtaining it."

Tabor murmurs out loud, "All we have to do now is figure out who they are."

Everyone turns to look at him, but he stands firm. The commander clearly believes this is the most important element to understand. After thinking it over for a minute, I decide he's not wrong. "Someone is targeting our females. Finding out who did this will lead us to the way to best stop them from future biological attacks." Looking from one to another of them, I can see understanding dawn on their faces. It makes my takadon's next request easier to accept. "Our best course of action is to bring Captain Artor out of stasis long enough for him to answer questions about where he obtained the elixir."

"It appears that fragments of the symbiont have been absorbed into his bloodstream. We can't take a chance on him spreading it by getting into a fight which might lead to open wounds." Stacy's warning is reflected in Phan's concerned expression.

I glance from Stacy to the blue-hued alien lying on the hovering healing platform. "If we want to discover who the evil scientists are, we need to do this. Maybe we can adjust the intensity of the stasis field or pull it back to a bubble around his unit."

Tabor walks over to one of the consoles and begins keying in commands. The moment the stasis field shimmers to life and pulls back, Captain Artor bolts forward into a sitting position. One leg comes up with his foot resting on the platform, and it looks for all the world like he's getting ready to push off the mat and attack us. Before I can speak, my takadon's voice rings out, deep and stern.

"Do not get off the healing platform, Captain Artor. If you do, we will be forced to stun you again. If you wish to remain alert and protect your queen, you must cooperate."

The alien's head snaps up, and he looks around the room, catching a glimpse of the woman he's been asking for lying on a nearby healing platform. He sucks in a horrified breath before screaming. "What have you done to my bride? Your quarrel is with me." His eyes are wild with shock and worry. Thinking better of making demands, he lowers his voice. I can tell he's trying to get his aggression under control. "Do not harm an innocent."

I speak up, trying to calm him. "We're not going to hurt either of you. You're both sick. The elixir you shared is poisoning you and allowing a vicious symbiont to take over your bride's mind."

His eyes flick back and forth between us and the woman he hopes to make his bride. "You lie. The priestesses of Kalafor would not deceive me."

"Who are these females you trust so much?"

Something akin to confusion and self-doubt crosses his expression. "They are one from each species, living in harmony. I paid them tribute, and they gifted me with the elixir. I was instructed to drink in front of them, and then go in search of my bride. Sharing with her will allow her to see past my rough exterior to my soul. I am a male of worth, and she will be gifted with the ability to see me as I truly am. The priestesses live in peace, because they have been gifted with the ability to see in other beings what they hide from themselves." As he talks, his voice rises. I suspect he realizes that he sounds thoroughly unhinged.

His voice slows, and he stammers "They said I was rare and worthy of…" He's sweating again and slowly begins to tremble. I don't realize there is a problem until Stacy and Phan move forward, quickly keying commands into the medical unit computer. "Lock the stasis field back down, there has been a huge jump in activity by the contaminant.

Tabor moves to do that, and the last thing I hear is Artor scream. "Save my queen. Do not let her die." The tone of his voice is strangled and rough, like he's losing his ability to talk. I'm certainly not an Artor fan but seeing him like that is horrifying. A hand lands on my shoulder, and my mother drapes her arm around me. It reminds me that she's probably stronger than I will ever be.

We stand there for a stunned moment, then Tabor walks over to me and takes me under his wing. I wrap my arms around his waist, as Scarn draws my mother back under his wing.

The always-silent Meric speaks. "We are on a clandestine mission to join with other species belonging to the Intergalactic Council of Planets. We have shared the limited information we have on the symbionts. Unfortunately, disturbing evidence has surfaced indicating that the symbionts might be attempting to breach our sector of space. This latest bit of intelligence from Artor might prove to be critical to helping us understand enough to eradicate the symbionts from our sector of space."

Stacy walked over to stand beside him. "We're putting together a team of the best medical professionals in the ICP. If there are no objections, I'm going to take these two patients with me. They are the first early-stage hosts we've encountered. They are unusual because the symbionts breached their bodies after being suspended in a liquid form. It's very much like how the Draconian queens are being infected in the Cave of Ascension in their sector of space."

I chimed in my two cents' worth. "It would be great if we could figure out how they're getting here from Exion space."

Phan held his data pad close. "If we knew the entry point, we could close it off."

Scarn drew my mother tighter into his embrace. His wings were drawn tight behind his back. "Though it pains me to say this, we owe the millions of our brethren in the Exion sector better than closing off their only avenue of escape. We should look for ways to liberate them."

My mother nodded her agreement. "It's really scary to know that any of us could be infected, but allowing an entire civilization of people to continue being enslaved by the symbionts is wrong. If we can offer any assistance at all, we should."

Kendra's voice calls from the doorway. "I agree. Phan and I should go with Stacy. He's a healer, and I can make myself useful."

Meric cuts her off at the pass. "Only a select few are invited to attend this convention. We are each to share knowledge and return home with a firm plan in place for battling the symbionts. You should return to our new home world and safely offload the multitude of queens you have acquired."

Stacy attempts to smooth over his rejection. "We don't want to do anything to get us excluded from these talks. They're kind of touchy because they think we brought this on them because the symbionts are from Draconian space."

Meric tried to turn the conversation in a different direction. "Word has reached our home world that there are little ones in need of homes. I am told there are more families eager to adopt than children in need. Your arrival will be met with much joy and celebration."

Phan shot Kendra a spectacular smile. "They're really adorable. I could play with them all day."

She grudgingly muttered, "I guess we'll take things a step at a time."

Our mother shifted the conversation back to family. "I would love to spend some time with my daughters and maybe get to know their love interests a little better before they go off onto another exciting mission."

"I can't argue with that. It would be nice to have some downtime before things get crazy-busy again." Tabor tugs me back to his chest and peers down into my face when I look up to catch his eye. His hands rub my belly, like he's trying to send me a secret message.

I can feel his wings wrapped around my shoulders, making me feel warm and connected. It takes me a moment to realize that I won't be participating in any crazy shenanigans anytime soon, because I might be pregnant. I stiffen as it occurs to me that if there is a possibility that I'm pregnant, his parthenogenesis must have ignited because his mating scent is gone.

I turn in his arms, and my hand drops to the lower right side of his abs, and sure enough, there are two little bumps. We're going to have young of our own. Draping my arm around his neck, I drag him down for a chaste kiss, whispering, "All I want is to get home and nest." I'm using his word for sleeping, but really I'm referring to my instinctive need to work on providing a home for my new family.

He runs his fingers through my hair. "I would see you safely tucked away in my home where no harm can come to us during our time of breeding." He's feeling the same way. My heart squeezes with emotion.

The word breeding has always rubbed me the wrong way, but right now I have to admit I'm warming right up to the word. Though it's the wrong time and place for romance, he dips his head and ghosts his lips across mine. I'm sure no one cares if we sneak a quick kiss, so I get lost for moment, enjoying every second until he pulls back. A self-satisfied smile tugs at the corners of his mouth.

Everyone else's conversation is background noise, as I gaze up into his handsome face. Reaching up, I trace the intricate pattern running down his cheek, trying to remember why I ever though the markings were sinister. His green skin and oversized eyes strike me as exotic and interesting. The symbols tracking down his body now seem whimsical and decorative, something that makes him unique. Even though there are some symbols that represent his clade, they are worked into an intricate design of his choosing. "I'm glad you're mine, my takadon."

Pressing his hand against my cheek, he whispers, "I would belong to no other."

Standing there face-to-face, we share a moment of awareness of how fragile our lives are. We just rescued my family and bunch of other vulnerable people from Earth and had it out with two of our most fearsome enemies. We need some downtime. It's strange how we're both on the same page so much of the time. It makes me think that we were meant to be.

ome World

~ Tabor ~

I watch the Strovian technicians carting off the rest of the high-tech device that folds space-time. I sign off that it has all been done properly by scanning my hand across the DNA reader. The technician scans his hand as well, and we each are sent a copy of the verification.

Elder Scarn speaks out behind me. "That was a bit more trouble than I anticipated."

I speak the only appropriate response that comes to mind. "The Strovians pride themselves on formality, uniformity, and precision. Making sure transactions are outlined in advance and executed properly seems in line with their values."

Scarn comes up beside me. "I suppose we are lucky they agree to use the device to bring us to our home world prior to removing it, rather than us being required to go to Strovia Prime to have it removed. All that travel would have taken months."

"It seems the Strovians value their superior programming over the loss of a single ship. They stripped out all the core programing from the ship and erased the programing from their soldiered bots."

Scarn tosses me a lopsided smile. "I can't say that was much of a loss. Their bots were poor fighters. We will program them for service functions, and be better off knowing they cannot harm females the moment our back is turned."

"We have techs from our home world installing new Draconian programming, even as we speak. I agree that our new ship will be safer without Strovian programming in our database."

"This ship is the largest in orbit. You must be proud of yourself and your queen for acquiring it."

"I am pleased none lost their lives in the attack. This ship is a nice trophy and will serve our people well, which brings me to our next order of business. The Grayson clan are intent on digging gemstone and purchasing their own vessel. What say you to taking our old ship?"

"The one you never named?" His gentle teasing about my over-sight does not sting, for both of us know there was no time for such unimportant tasks. "I never saw myself as captain material," he says.

"You have a queen. She will wish her own space and authority over her own warriors. This you can provide by sitting in the captain's seat with her at your side."

Rubbing his chin, Scarn ponders my words. "I think my intended queen wishes to care for, rather than have authority over warriors. She might wish to be equal to her daughters by having her own ship."

"Let us set the wishes of queens aside for a moment, my friend. We both have people we wish to protect. Your level of experience far outweighs that of any warrior I know. I would ask you to take command of the secondary vessel, so that together we might protect the queens and the young we make with them."

"When you put it like that, I can hardly think of a worthy reason to reject your offer."

Slapping him on the shoulder, I speak my heart. "It is my honor to have you in my family and at my side in battle, Elder Scarn."

"I live to serve, Commander Tabor."

"As do all warriors, my friend. You are in good company."

We part, with my duties for the day finished and Elder Scarn's just beginning. Excitement strums through my body so strongly, that I can barely refrain from flying back to our new quarters. I know my sweet queen is there, unpacking and sorting through the multitude of purchases I made on Earth for our new home. She will create a spacious suite for us to nest in upon this vessel, and another, more elaborate nest on the planet below. I would have my beautiful queen and young be comfortable in whatever environment commands our attention.

She is just ushering some of the warriors away with the items she intends to use on our new home world. They have multiple hover boards loaded with our belongings, and their heads dip respectfully as they pass by me to get to the door. Their softly murmured greetings cause my queen to look up. The moment her soft blue eyes meet mine, a brilliant smile lights up her face. "It pleases me that you always seem so happy to see me, my queen."

"What's not to like? I spent way too long denying myself your company." Her voice is sincere and admiring. She honestly likes me, not my pretty face or all the things I do to serve her. She likes me as a male. When other warriors tried to explain to me about love and bonding with a human queen, I did not understand. It is something I believe one must experience to truly comprehend. Since I am lost in my own thought and not responding to her fast enough, my queen rises from the box she is going through and closes the distance between us quickly. "What's wrong? Did your meeting with the Strovian technicians not go according to plan?"

I reach out and draw her into my arms. I do not wish to talk about work. "Yes, it all went according the plan we outlined with them. Nothing is wrong. I sometimes get lost in my own thoughts. It is an old and troublesome habit. I never thought to be selected by a queen, and yet here I am with the most desirable queen on the planet as my mate. It seems so impossible to believe, that I worry this is all just a dream."

She relaxes in my arms and cuddles herself close with her cheek on my chest. I know she likes this position because she can hear my hearts beating.

"I know exactly what you mean. I used to have nightmares of waking up back on Earth with all my family lying around dead on the ground. Sometimes my dreams were filled with images of us being forced to do awful things to survive."

Cupping her under the chin with one hand, I gently tilt her head up so I can look into her eyes. "Tell me you no longer have such terrible dreams."

"I rarely have those types of dreams anymore, especially since you've been my bed warmer."

I can't help but smile that she uses her mother's teasing descriptor for Scarn to refer to me. I squeeze one of her hands, and then bring it down to the palm-sized swell where our twins are growing. I know it is bragging to point out so boldly that I am growing young for her, but she seems to love being reminded. Her soft hand slides over my tender flesh, reminding me how different we are in that regard. I am hard muscle and thick skin, whereas she is delicate and sensual. My roughness turns her on, and so does my ability to breed young for her. I know my new queen is fertile, and soon her belly will swell with our child as well. The thought of having three healthy young fills me with pride and anticipation.

When my queen drops to her knees in front of me, my heart nearly stops. I have never even once in my lifetime seen a queen kneeling before a warrior. It simply is not done. Before I can beg her to rise, her hands are on my uniform, pulling it open. The magnetic seams around my shoulders give, and it falls down from around my wings. I have some idea of what she is doing, because it is something warriors sometimes pay for in brothels. I believe she intends to put her mouth upon me, and when she pulls the uniform down to reveal my eager cock, I decide I wish for this more than anything.

My wings unfurl, and in my moment of weakness, I do not care. Every thought is burned from my mind when her hand wraps around my stiff cock. I cannot stop looking down at her. The skin around my groin is slightly darker, and seeing my dark green flesh sliding in and out of her fist makes my knees weak.

"You're really a handful. Hold still, okay babe?"

"All will be as you wish, my queen."

"Oh no, this is about you having all that you wish." With that pronouncement, she leans forward and licks the head of my cock. Seeing her pink tongue moving over me that way makes it impossible to breathe. She sucks me inside her mouth. With no hope of taking all of me, she begins to suck. The warriors describe this act as the pinnacle of sexual pleasure, next to being inside a female, of course. I must agree that this is amazing, particularly because it is a gift straight from the heart of my very own queen, and not something I paid a stranger to do.

She takes one of my hands and tangles it in her hair. Shock rolls through me when takes her hand away and becomes still. What she is offering seems to be too good to be true, yet I know my queen would never lead me astray. Pulling her head by her hair, I look down into her eyes. Her submission is unmistakable. I crave control, and my queen enjoys submitting. I loosen my hold and rock myself gently against her tongue. She begins to swirl her tongue around my tip each time I pull back. When my pace quickens, her hands come up to caress all the sensitive places on my body that she can reach. She's making tiny sounds of pleasure, and I am careful not to abuse the power she has given me. The idea of choking a queen on my cock is revolting. Everything else about this situation is pure pleasure.

When the scent of her pheromones fills the air, I can no longer control myself. I pull out, lift her into the air and splay her legs across my face. My tongue seeks out what I crave and both her hands land on my horns to steady her position. It is a good thing they are as stiff as my cock right now. I let myself go wild, teasing and sucking her tender bud until she screams my name. Then I slide her right down my body and onto my cock.

She's totally lost in the pleasure looping back and forth between us. Her eyes are closed, and she's whispering compliments and words of encouragement. This queen was made just for me. I shove her down onto the nearby sleeping platform and come down hard on top of her. Rather than complaint, I get a wide-eyed stare of absolute passion.

When I begin using her roughly, her hands come up to rub up and down my back, teasing my wing base with each down stroke. This lovely queen knows all the spots that arouse my passion the most, and she is not afraid to use them. It is one of the things I like best about her.

I shift my body to rub all the right places and she detonates beneath me. As always when she locks down around me, it drags me over the edge with her. I empty my seed deep inside her soft, quivering body and pray one hits the mark. That is assuming that one hasn't already done so during one of our previous lovemaking sessions. My queen has not had much time for such pursuits in her life. It is my honor and pleasure to make up for that oversight.

I curl around her, and we look into each other's eyes. "Are you well, my sensual and dedicated queen?"

Barely able to get her breath, she responds, "I'm better than well, my energetic and always-ready Takadon."

I chuckle, still a bit breathless as well. "I am honored and pleased by your gift, my queen."

Rolling over to face me, she gives me an exhausted smile. "That wasn't a gift. It was just a normal part of having sexy time."

"I appreciate every single moment of time you choose to spend in my arms. Before we escaped the rule of the queens, no warrior had any hope of experiencing a loving touch from a female. You can't know the hardship we endured."

"I can well imagine how it must have been. The hardship is written in the scars that cover Scarn and Meric, as well as in your own reluctance to accept advances from a woman."

Pulling her to my chest, I muse out loud. "I wonder what the warriors still trapped under the rule of Draconian queens are doing. Queen Hope educated them about the symbionts before we left. They either instigated a full-scale revolt, or were killed before they could pass the information on."

"Let's appreciate the joy and happiness we've fought so hard to secure and think on your brethren another day. I have a feeling war with the queens of old is brewing. If that is the case, Meric will see that all the member worlds of the Intergalactic Council of Planets fight in one unified block."

Rubbing her back, I realize for the first time our people have a real chance of throwing off the control of the symbionts. "There are millions of warriors aching to be free."

My queen looks over her shoulder at me, and I can see the love in her eyes, right alongside a fierce loyalty to my kind. "My world has millions of females with no hope of ever finding love. We've got to have faith. That isn't some strange coincidence. It means that like you and me, they are fated to one another."

"Is this what you really think? I thought you believe in making one's destiny."

Snuggling back down beside me, her voice floats to my ears. "I believe the gods guide us, but we must make our own choices and live with the consequences. I risked everything to rescue my family and was rewarded with a fine mate. Perhaps it will be the same with your brethren and my fellow humans."

I think over my queen's words, and determine that she is likely right. I operated in good faith and ended up with a kind and generous queen. Why should it be any different for the other warriors?

Relaxing into the moment, my head swirls with memories of my life before and my life now. Before there was only darkness, pain,

deprivation and the misery of watching our queens destroy innocent planets. Draconian queens never gave a care for the loss of a
warrior. There were no special words or commemorations of the
male's sacrifice.

On our new home world, the queens treat us as equals. They
seem as dedicated to our needs as we are to theirs. My queen
sensed my desire was to wield control, so she puts me in command
of her ship and our lovemaking. Was ever a warrior so honored by
his queen? I vow in this moment to wield such control benevo-
lently, just as the human queens do over all the warriors. My
glorious queen leads the way, and I am honored to follow.

Lifting her leg gently, I nudge her opening with my cock.
Thinking of my queen's many fine qualities has aroused my interest
in mating again. I hear a small, playful laugh and she pushes back,
impaling herself on my cock. I waste no time taking what my queen
has offered, knowing that her warm body and scent are all I ever
want. Sliding into her body equals sliding home for me. Having this
small human queen in my arms is all in the 'verse I will ever need to
find true peace and happiness.

THE END

Keep reading for more Draconian Warrior Adventures - *Alien
Hero's Claimed Bride* is available now!

GLOSSARY

Akes – Draconian god of hunting, war and violence. He is the consort to Entares, the benevolent goddess worshiped by Draconian males.

Antar – Right (Lutar is left.)

Avada – Small carrot-like vegetable that is seasoned and wrapped in a dry leaf.

Challenge–Draconian queens settle disagreements and property disputes by challenging one another in single combat. It is usually a battle to the death.

Clade – Group of Draconians who are descended from a common set of genetic code.

Dark Star – Another term for black hole.

Doma – Type of Draconian flatbread.

Dracon Two – The name the second wave of Draconian warriors nicknamed Onello, which is their new home world in the Naxis sector of space.

Draconian - Species created by mixing dragon DNA with humanoid DNA. There are many family lines with unique strengths and weaknesses.

Entares – Draconian goddess of beauty, peace, and joy. The

males worship her as she represents their desire for females to show kindness and respect to them for their many sacrifices, rather than the harsh treatment they normally receive.

Exion – Vast Sector of space encompassing the Draconian home world. Exion is ruled by a race of ruthless females bent on conquest and power.

Hatching – Draconian method of reproduction by which warriors conceive and carry eggs.

Hatchling – Noun: Child. Hatching is a verb: Act of creating young by a male Draconian. Males hatch many times during their lifetimes.

Hatch Mate – Refers to only the children hatched during the same cycle of breeding.

Laser Pistol –A weapon used in battles and self-defense which uses power packs to fire short laser bursts.

Lutar - Left. (Antar is Right)

Moltan – Malevolent aliens who attack and destroy other vessels.

Naxis – Vast sector of space encompassing five galaxies, including the Milky Way.

Obsidian – The name of a Draconian ship.

Parsec – Unit of distance. Used mostly in determining distance in space.

Parthenogenesis – Draconians males undergo parthenogenesis when exposed to a female's pheromones. It results them incubating eggs in their bodies, which are released into specially designed incubators.

Phase Grenade – Device that sticks to the hull of a ship and disables their weapons.

Raspian – The second mother ship and one Hope and Larok use for the voyage to Onello.

Revidian – The word used by Draconians to denote a warrior performing oral sex on a queen.

Scion – A word used for offspring, no matter the age.

Strovian – Race of warriors who are at peace with the Draconians in the Naxis sector.

Takadon – The Draconian word for a male who is chosen to be the queen's primary breeder. He is to stay at her side constantly and is her protector.

Taladar – Species who initiated a trade agreement with Earth to exchange much-needed food and other supplies for human brides.

Tankea – Draconian word meaning love between a parent and child or between siblings.

Unders – Anything worn under one's uniform or regular clothing.

Tricon – Unit of thickness.

Utaka Larva – Pupa stage of growth for a tiny colorful flying creatures the Draconians keep for pets.

Vithacan – Symbionts that attach themselves to other creatures and survive off their emotional energy. Soul suckers is a disrespectful term for their race.

Zelerians – Race of squid-like creatures with few humanoid features.